TOM GATES

SPECTACULAR
SCHOOL TRIP (Really...)

By Liz Pichon

SCHOLASTIC

HUGE THANK YOU to

Neal Foster for bringing TOM GATES to the stage.

And everyone at the Birmingham Stage Company including the whole cast and crew.

You are all AWESOME!

Louise * Roshni * Kate * Adrian * Jackie * Jason T *
Matt * Nick * Nia * Daisy * Simon W * Matthew H *
Simon G * Joe * Heather * Charles * Ben * Dan *
Cecile * Maisie * Nicole * Matthew C * Daniel *
Alice * Harry S * Matthew G * Ashley * Amy *
Justin * Ebony

Love LIZ xx

Special thanks to SAM x

PETE and JASON x

ANDREW and CLAIRE x

LYN x

MARK F x

And to ALL of TEAM SCHOLASTIC, thank you for your hard work!

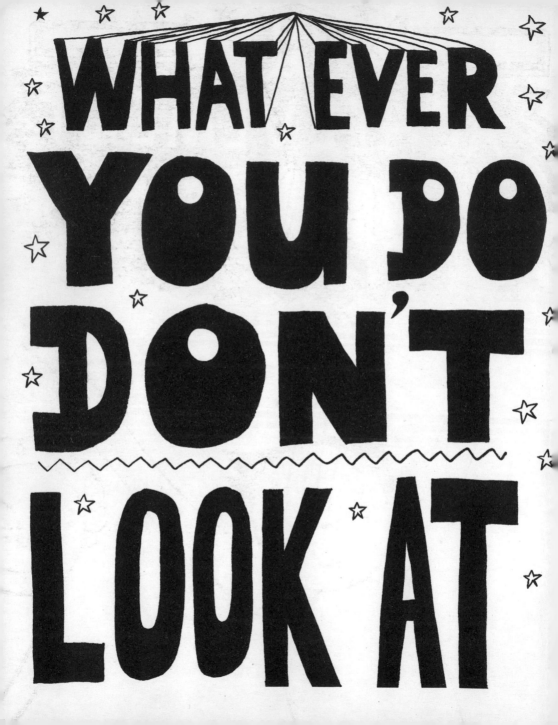

It's not like I MEANT to get THREE SAD FACES 😕 😕 😕. It just sort of happened.

MARCUS didn't help much. ➡️ He's only got ONE sad face. 😕

(Or two if you count his ACTUAL face.)

AND the worst part is, <u>NONE</u> of them were my fault.

It's true!

I got THIS ➡️ 😕 sad face in quiet time.

I was just doodling a nice picture of Mr Fullerman

with BIG EYES, TEETH and HAIR (lots of it)

when Marcus Meldrew (who's a nosey parker) started LAUGHING SO LOUDLY.

Ha! Ha! Ha! Ha!

You'll get in trouble if Mr Fullerman sees that!

"Shhhhhhhhhhhhhh! He won't see it if you keep QUIET!" I said... (Too late.)

Awww

TOM!
That's ONE SAD FACE for you!

(See what I mean? NOT my fault.)

THEN last week I was round at Derek's house getting my homework done ON TIME (for a change) when Rooster jumped up

GRABBED IT THEN RAN OFF.

Mr Fullerman was NOT impressed.

So let me get this right – the DOG ATE your homework AGAIN?

"YES, SIR," I said. "IT'S TRUE!"

That's your SECOND sad face of the term, Tom.

"AWWWWWWWWWWW."

(I couldn't believe I had two sad faces.)

THEN this morning I WOKE up REALLY EARLY for school and went to meet Derek, who was surprised to see me ON TIME.

Tom, you're here!

"Don't sound so surprised. Come on, LET'S GO. We don't want to be LATE!" I said.

Derek and I did *FAST WALKING* and tried not to get distracted by ANYTHING.

Then Derek suddenly stopped and shouted...

WHY NOT HAVE A WAFER?

WAFER

Hey, Tom! Look what I've found - 50p!

We did a high-five  and went straight to the shop. BUT deciding what to buy was TRICKY.

Hmmm   Hmmm

Should we get ...
ONE packet of cheesy **PUFFS**
and TWO fruit chews?

Or how about ONE caramel
wafer to share?

Maybe a WHOLE bag
of broken biscuits?

Derek suggested, which was a good idea.
BUT the shopkeeper spotted us checking which
bag was the biggest and said.

"Come on, you two - they're all the same SIZE."

(They're NOT the same size.

EVERYBODY knows that.)

While I checked the bags, Derek spotted that the LATEST copy of ROCK WEEKLY had DUDE 3 on the COVER.

Tom, look at this!

SO we took a sneaky peek through the WHOLE magazine while the queue went down, then decided to buy ONE caramel wafer (to share).

"It's a good plan," Derek agreed.

BUT when we got to the front of the queue, all the wafers had GONE, which was a

DISASTER.

NOOOOOOOO!

Luckily the shopkeeper SAVED the day and found another box, so we got a wafer after all.

"That's a relief," Derek said, and I agreed.

I split the wafer in two and enjoyed eating it slowly.

The trouble was we spent so much time in the shop that we missed the start of SCHOOL!

Ding! Ding! Ding! Ding! Ding!

Uh-oh...

"You're LATE, Tom. That's THREE SAD faces now."

"But, SIR!", I say in a "please don't give me another sad face" kind of way.

"If you get ONE more sad face, Tom, do you know what will happen?" Mr Fullerman asks.

"Sort of, sir..." I reply.

Then Marcus sticks up his hand and starts saying, "SIR! SIR! I know what will happen."

(Marcus is so annoying.)

"He'll get a DETENTION, sir, AND he'll have to do LOTS of extra homework, too."

"Thanks for reminding me, Marcus," I say.

Anytime... ← (Smug)

"You can put your hand down, Marcus. Right down. As I was saying, ANYONE with FOUR SAD FACES ☹ will NOT be allowed to go on the SCHOOL TRIP," Mr Fullerman tells us.

"SCHOOL TRiP? WHAT SCHOOL TRIP?" I ask.

"The school trip that YOU won't be going on with your **FOUR SAD FACES**," 😞 Marcus says.

So I point out, "I don't have FOUR sad faces, Marcus."

YET, he adds.

Quiet down! I'll tell you more about the school trip later. Right now here's something else to look forward to ... this week's homework.

"AWWWWWWWWWWWWWWWWWW," we all groan.

"It's VERY SPECIAL HOMEWORK," Mr Fullerman says, trying to make it sound interesting.

Like that even exists... I whisper to **AMY**.

"It's going to be displayed for the school OPEN day, when parents and carers come to look around our FANTASTIC SCHOOL and see if their own children would love it here. And who wouldn't want to come to Oakfield School, right, Class 5F?"

(S I L E N C E .)

Then Marcus sticks up his hand and says, "SIR! SIR! I can tell them how GREAT this school is."

"That's excellent, Marcus. I'm sure we can all think of lovely things to say about the school."

(S I L E N C E .)

15

"And I can tell them ALL about the achievement chart and how you can't EVER go on a school trip if you have THREE SAD FACES, 😞 sir," Marcus says, looking at me.

"It's actually FOUR sad faces, Marcus," Mr Fullerman corrects him.

"I think it should be THREE, sir, because THREE sad faces means you haven't been very good at all. And THREE is my LUCKY number," Marcus replies.

"You can't change the rules, Marcus," AMY tells him.

(Marcus is trying to stop me going on the school trip. But that's not going to happen.)

"Now, Class 5F, listen carefully. Your HOMEWORK is ..."

I hope it's not going to be HARD. I can't get another sad face for getting it wrong,

I whisper.

Then Mr Fullerman says,

"That reminds me, Tom, I know you like drawing and doodling."

"Sometimes, sir..."

"Well, the council have created a special DOODLE WALL just for kids like you to draw on."

"That's AMAZING! Where is it, sir?"

"The address is on this leaflet. The council wants to encourage children to be CREATIVE and draw in this one special place where it's allowed – so it's NOT graffiti."

Mr Fullerman passes out leaflets showing where the wall is.

WOW! My homework is a **POSTER** and there's an actual doodle wall to draw on, too. How **GOOD** is that? Though **AMY** doesn't look that happy. (Marcus looks the same as usual.)

"I can't wait to go to the *DOODLE WALL*. How about you?" I ask **AMY**.

"I'm not bothered. Drawing's not my thing," she tells me so I say, "Come on, **AMY** – ANYONE can draw. Even Marcus can doodle. Look. Don't ask me what it is, though," I point out as Marcus is busy.

"I think I'll go to the wall after school and draw **THIS**. It's good, isn't it?" Marcus shows us his drawing.

"What is it?" **AMY** asks.

"Isn't it **OBVIOUS**?" Marcus sighs.

"A SELF PORTRAIT?" I say.

"Very funny, Tom. I'm going to be the first person to draw on the doodle wall. Then everyone will see how good I am," he boasts.

"What happens if I get there BEFORE you, Marcus?" I ask him.

"You won't, Tom, because you're LATE for everything. AND that's why you've got FOUR sad faces." 😧😧😧😧

"Actually, I've only got THREE sad faces," I correct him.

"FOR NOW..." he adds, smiling.

Then AMY says,

"Maybe I will go to the wall after all. I can copy your doodle style, Tom, if that's OK?"

"Sure..." I say, slightly surprised.

Marcus covers his work.

"Don't even think about copying MY style."

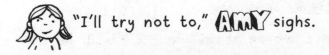

"I'll try not to," AMY sighs.

"Hey, Tom – can you do one of your doodles?" she wonders. So I write my name and draw around it.

"Whoa! You're so *FAST.* That's great!"

AMY says when I finish.

"Hmmmmm... It's not that good,"

Marcus grumbles. We ignore him.

"Why don't we all go to the **DOODLE WALL** after school together with Derek? I'm sure one of my parents will drive us," I say confidently.

(I hope they will.)

"I'm in!" AMY tells me.

"I'm OUT, but don't worry about me – I'll still be at the wall before BOTH of you," Marcus says smugly.

"**N**o one's worried about you, Marcus,"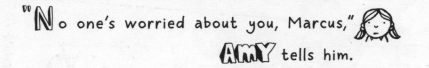
AMY tells him.

"My drawings are **AMAZING**, aren't they?"

"YES, Marcus — you're a genius," I say.

Sigh

"I know!"

He's not, but sometimes it's just easier to agree. Besides, I've got far more important things to think about now, LIKE...

1. Going to the *DOODLE WALL* after school.

2. Telling Derek that we're going to the *DOODLE WALL* so he can come too.

3. Doing my poster homework EARLY.

4. Impressing Mum and Dad with my EARLY poster homework so they'll drive us to the *DOODLE WALL.*

5. Getting a good after-school SNACK.

(That might be at the TOP of my list, if I'm honest.)

Once I'm home, I get BUSY with my homework, which seems to SURPRISE Mum.

"Hi, Tom. You _do_ know you're missing **CRAZY FRUIT BUNCH** on TV right now, don't you?"

"Thanks, Mum, but I'm doing my homework EARLY," I say, hoping she'll be super IMPRESSED!

"WOW, well done. I'm impressed!"

RESULT

"Did I just hear you say you were doing your homework EARLY, Tom?" Dad asks.

"YES! I've nearly finished it too. A little hard work NEVER hurt anyone."

I can't believe I just said THAT. But I really want to get to the doodle wall before Marcus does.

"It's all down to good parenting," Dad whispers.

"Mum, Dad..."

"Yes, Tom?"

"As I've finished my homework {EARLY} and I'm your FAVOURITE CHILD, can you take me to the NEW *DOODLE WALL?*"

"A *DOODLE WALL?* Isn't that just graffiti?" Dad asks.

"No, it's official. Mr Fullerman gave us a leaflet, see? Everyone's going after school," I explain.

"I don't see why not, Tom," Mum says.

"I can take you in the new car."

 "We have a NEW car?"
Mum sounds surprised.

"Just for a week. It's for a job I'm working on,"
Dad explains quickly.

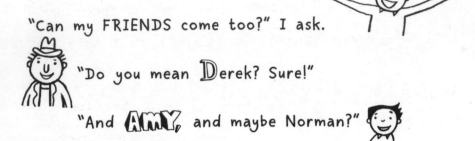

"Can my FRIENDS come too?" I ask.

 "Do you mean Derek? Sure!"

"And AMY, and maybe Norman?"

"Why not?" Dad agrees.

"THANKS, MUM AND DAD! You're the BEST parents ever!"

(It always helps to say things like that, along with
"PLEASE," "Thank you," and "Mmmmmm,
this broccoli is delicious!")

We all stop to listen to a strange **NOISE** that's coming from outside.

RUMBLE

"I have a FEELING that could be your grandparents come for a visit!" Mum tells us.

"YEAH! It's THE FOSSILS!" I shout because sometimes they bring TREATS!

"HELLO! We're HERE!" Granddad cheers, and Granny Mavis says, "We've brought CAKE!"

Yum...

"... with ONION sprinkles on TOP," she adds, "and a cheeky little cucumber filling!"

Errrr...

Oh...

"It's so PACKED with goodness, it's one of your FIVE a day!" Granny tells us.

Onion sprinkles

Cucumber filling

Suspicious bits in cake

"Let me cut you a NICE BIG SLICE!"

"That's OK, Granny. I've already eaten."

"You have?"

"Um, yes – a bit. But I don't want to get full before dinner and RUIN my appetite."
(Or my stomach – THE FOSSILS like VERY odd combinations of food.)

← Pasta
← Cheese
← Melon

"I'll save you a piece for later, Tom," Granny tells me.

"It is a CELEBRATION cake after all."

"Ooh! What are we celebrating then?" Mum asks.

"We've got a date for your diary!" Granddad says.

"We decided to GET MARRIED all over AGAIN!" Granny smiles.

"You have? WHO TO?" I ask.

"To EACH OTHER, of course!"

"Don't be so sure, Bob. I mean, you are getting on a bit." Granny LAUGHS.

"HA! Your granny's HILARIOUS – and that's why I can't wait to RENEW our wedding vows."

"We came by to check you've still got the special GATES FAMILY HAT."

"There's a FAMILY hat?" I ask.

"Yes, it's a lovely old top hat, Tom!" Granny tells me.

"It's been in the family for years and years. I wore it on our wedding day and my father wore it on his wedding day," Granddad explains.

"That hat is a PRECIOUS family heirloom," Granny adds.

"Errrr ... so EXACTLY how precious is it?" I check.

VERY PRECIOUS.

"That's SO exciting! You two are FULL of surprises," Mum says cheerily. "I think the hat's in a trunk upstairs. I'll go and get it."

"We're going to have some FUN, Tom. I'm even writing a poem to read at the ceremony!" Granddad smiles.

"And I'm making ALL the food!" Granny adds.

"ALL of it, Granny?" I ask.

"Yes! Don't look so worried, Tom. I'll definitely have lots of your favourite treats."

"Like CARAMEL WAFERS?"

"Even better than that! There'll be FISH BISCUITS."

(It could be worse, I suppose.)

Vegetable biscuits

"I might need to brush up on my SPOONS for the entertainment as well - what do you think?" Granddad starts playing a pair of teaspoons like an EXPERT.

"Better than playing your TEETH, Bob!" Granny LAUGHs.

"OH! I can do that as well!"

"Don't you dare..." Granny warns him.

At that exact moment, Delia comes home.

"Guess what, Delia?" I say.

What?

"Your grandparents are renewing their wedding vows and having a party too.

Isn't that GREAT?" Dad tells her.

Thrilling... Delia grumbles.

), "Look, I've found the hat!" Mum says as she comes back. "Oh, hello, Delia. Have you heard the GOOD NEWS?"

"Can't you tell? Look how happy she is!" I joke.

"And you're here just in time for my NEXT TRICK!" Granddad says and then takes his teeth OUT.

Click
Clack
Clickity
Clack

(Delia is not impressed.)

"Could you **ALL** just pretend to be a **NORMAL** family for once? I've got someone important coming over."

"Not Avril?" I groan. (Avril is Delia's friend.)

"No..." Delia tells me.

"Who's so important then?" I want to know.

"No one you know..."

"Is it your boyfriend?" I say as that drives her crazy. Then Mum says,

"A boyfriend?"

"No...

What's the point? No one ever listens to me," Delia grumbles and stomps out of the kitchen. Delia's in a particularly grumpy mood.  Though to be fair, she's not that keen on lots of things like:

1) SMILING 2) SUNLIGHT 3) HAVING FUN.

"Bob, put your teeth back in. You can't eat without them," Granny says.

"Good point..." he agrees.

"Now, who's in for a NICE slice of cake? And I won't take NO for an answer." (Granny's looking at me.)

Uh-oh.

This seems like a good time to head to the **DOODLE WALL,** as I have to get there before Marcus.

HERE

"Um, maybe later, Granny," I smile, then I tell Dad I'm ready to go when he is.

"OK, Tom. I won't be long – I've just got to pick up the new car. I'll have some cake later, Mavis." (He won't) "Tom, keep an eye out for me," Dad says.

"But what does the car look like?" I call after him.

Yellow...

While I'm KEEPING WATCH out of the
window, Delia walks past. I take the opportunity
to have another NICE little chat.
(Delia LOVES it when I ask her questions.) ☺

"DELIA!" I shout.

What now?

"Why do you wear sunglasses all the time?"

"So I can BLOCK out things that annoy me."

"WHY?"

"Because you're annoying."

"WHY?"

"WHY?"

"I know you can hear me!"

"Mum and Dad said I can have a

PET."

"**TWO** pets, actually, with LOADS of **FUR**. <u>AND</u> I'm getting a drum kit so I can practise right next to your bedroom."

"The other day I used **YOUR** hairbrush on ROOSTER. He looked LOVELY and smooth after."

"You better NOT have used my hairbrush, Tom!"

"**SEE?** I <u>KNEW</u> you were listening!"

(I <u>did</u> use her hairbrush, but I'm not going to admit that now.)

"Why are you hanging around by the door anyway? Haven't you got something better to do?" she wants to know.

"<u>N</u>ot really – besides I'm waiting for Dad to bring the NEW car around.

He's taking me and my friends to the ***DOODLE WALL...***"

"A ***DOODLE WALL?***" Delia repeats.

"Yes. It's a special wall just for doodles. I could draw a BIG picture of YOU on it?"

"DON'T YOU DARE or I'll tell Dad that you pinched <u>ALL</u> his biscuits from the shed."

"No, I didn't!"

(I did – but not ALL of them.)

"How LONG are you going to be standing here for?"

"WHY?"

"<u>Don't</u> start that again. <u>LISTEN</u> – if the doorbell goes, <u>I'LL</u> answer it, not you. I'm expecting someone. OK?"

"WHO?" I want to know.

"Never mind – just <u>don't</u> answer the door."

Delia stomps off, so I keep looking out for Dad. I wish he'd hurry up. I don't want Marcus to get to the wall before us. Then the bell suddenly goes.

So I ANSWER it before Delia comes back.

(Of course I do...)

"Hello? Can I help you?" I say to the bloke who's at the door.

"Hi. Is Delia home?"

"Are you her BOYFRIEND? Because __IF__ you are I think I should SHARE a few interesting __FACTS__ about her with you," I say helpfully. "After all I'm her little brother, so I know stuff."

"Oh, actually, I just want to..."

"For instance, when Delia was younger she had a lot of NITS. So I wouldn't get too close to her if I were you. You __NEVER__ know, they could still be there."

(I scratch a bit to demonstrate how bad it can get.)

"Um..."

"The thing is..."

"Also," I interrupt him, "Delia likes to pretend that she's really cool but I know for a FACT she LOVES One Dimension - they're her favourite band EVER."

"You mean One Dimension, the boy band?"

"Yes! She's got posters of them all over her walls." I smile.

(It's fun to watch the expression on his face.)

Really?

She does.

"What else do you want to know?"

"Is Delia in a band?" he asks.

"Hmmm... Not that I know of. I'm the one in the band. We're called **DOGZOMBIES** but we need to practise more," I say.

"Yeah, you gotta keep practising if you're in a band," he says. "I'm in a band as well. Which reminds me, can you give this note to your sister? It's very important she gets it," the bloke tells me.

"Ewwwwwww – it's not a love letter, is it?" I ask suspiciously.

"No, it's not. Can you just..."

He's interrupted by a LOUD car horn that BLASTS OUT!

TAH DAH DA DA! TAH DAH DA DA! TAH DAH DA DA! TAH DAH DA DA!

"Whoa! Can you see that CAR?" I shout.

"It's hard not to," he agrees.

"That's my dad driving!" I explain. "Hey, what's your band called? He might have heard of it. Dad loves talking about bands!"

"I doubt it. Just give that to Delia, will you? Thanks!" he tells me then disappears *fast.*

TAH DAH DA DA! TAH DAH DA DA!

I'm OFF...

"Don't say I didn't WARN you about Delia," I remind him and go to look at the car when Dad presses the horn AGAIN.

TAH DAH DA DA! TAH DAH DA DA! TAH DAH DA DA!
(It's impressive.)

"He didn't say his name, but he's in a band...
ANYWAY, this car's BRILLIANT!
Where did you get it from?" I ask.

"Isn't it great? It belongs to a cafe I'm doing some
work for," Dad says as Mum comes out for a look.

"PLEASE tell me that's not our new car?"

she says.

"I can tell you're excited," Dad says, which doesn't make Mum laugh. "It's not for long – we've only got it for a bit," he adds. Then Delia comes outside and she's even MORE PLEASED than Mum. (Not.)

"ARE YOU SERIOUS?
This is SO EMBARRASSING. Can you please just GO before anyone sees it?" Delia tells Dad.

"It's a bit late for that,"
Mum says, rolling her eyes.

(I still think it's FANTASTIC.)

Then Derek comes *RUNNING* over looking happier than all of us.
"Tom! Tom! Are we going to the
DOODLE WALL in that car?" he wants to know.
"Yes, we are, Derek..." I say.

"THAT'S THE BEST CAR EVER!"

Derek shouts.

(I think he likes the car.)

"Jump in, boys. We can collect your other friends on the way," Dad tells us.

"Make sure you go the RIGHT way, Frank. You don't want to get stuck under a bridge with that HOT DOG," Mum tells Dad as we get ready to leave.

"Good point, Rita. Come on, boys. Have you both got something to draw with?"

"Check!" we both say as Derek's brought a stack of good pens.

"I've got my poster homework to copy from too!" It's a good job I finished it early. This will be SUPER USEFUL.

"EXCELLENT. Now off we go! Nice and quietly, just blending in..." Dad tells us happily. We pick up Norman and AMY on the way. They are almost as impressed with the car as Derek was.

Dad says it won't take long to get to the **DOODLE WALL.** But we've been driving around for AGES.

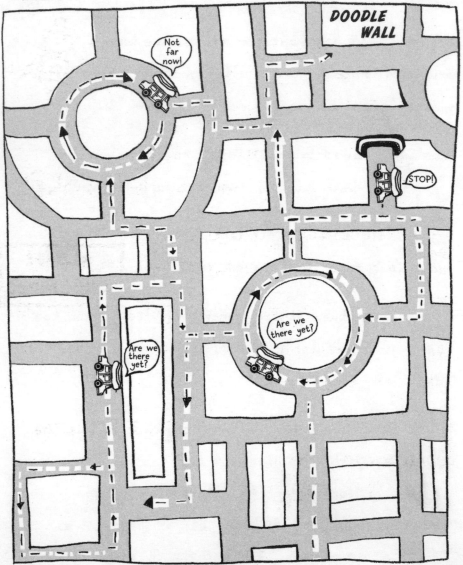

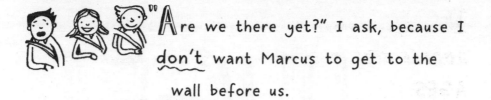"Are we there yet?" I ask, because I don't want Marcus to get to the wall before us.

"Nearly!" Dad says, but I'm sure we've been down this road before. I wait another whole minute before asking again...

"It's just down this road," Dad says, which is a MISTAKE!

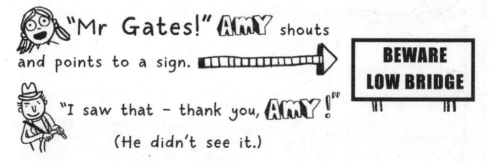"Mr Gates!" AMY shouts and points to a sign.

BEWARE LOW BRIDGE

"I saw that – thank you, AMY!"

(He didn't see it.)

Finally, Dad stops the car.

"We're here! According to the leaflet, THIS is the

DOODLE WALL!"

We all jump out of the car and *RUSH* to the wall, which is **HUGE.**

"Where do we start?" Norman asks excitedly.

"Tom, YOU said you'd show us how to doodle in your style," AMY reminds me.

"I did, and I brought my poster homework to HELP."

I proudly take out my poster homework and show everyone.

"I like the way you drew those patterns and put  sunglasses on a monster. That's funny!" AMY LAUGHs.

"Oh, that's my sister, Delia. Though she can be  quite scary," I explain.

"It's true,"  Derek agrees with me.

"I might draw her on the wall anyway..." I say.

"Your drawings are GREAT, Tom!" AMY tells me  (which is nice).

DRAWING LANE

"Mr Fullerman will definitely get rid of one of your sad faces now," AMY carries on saying,

and Dad hears her.

"What sad faces, Tom?" he wants to know.

"Errr... It's nothing, Dad," I say quickly.

"I've got TWO sad faces 🙁 🙁," Norman chips in.

"I've got NO sad faces as I'm not in Tom's class," Derek adds.

"I've got THREE smiley faces 🙂 🙂 🙂," AMY tells Dad happily.

(Which doesn't help me much.)

"So how many SAD faces 🙁 do you have then, Tom? Dad wants to know.

"Umm..."

"I don't think anyone's really counting, Dad," I try and explain.

"That's not totally true, Tom. Remember what Mr Fullerman told us about the SAD FACES?" 😟 AMY says.

"No," I say, hoping we can move on. Then Norman JUMPS UP and does an impression of Mr Fullerman. "I do! He said ANYONE with FOUR sad faces WON'T be allowed on the SCHOOL TRIP!"

Then Dad asks, "Is that right, Tom?"

"Yes ... but the GOOD NEWS is because I've done my poster homework early, that's not going to happen. Shall we do some doodling NOW?" I say, and we get going.

Doodling on the wall (before Marcus) is EXTRA **FUN.** Then Derek says, "Hey, have you noticed we're DRAWING on Drawing Lane? How weird is that?"

Then **AMY** says, "No – it's Drawing Road."

"But this is Drawing Lane, see?" Derek says and he points to the sign.

AMY gets out the leaflet to have another look.
"I'm just going to show this to your dad," she says.
I carry on with my doodle and add my name so
Marcus can see it when he arrives. (I'm taking up a
lot of space!)

As I'm doodling, a lady comes up to me.

"What's going on here, then?" she asks.

 "It's the NEW council doodle wall.
It's **GREAT**, isn't it?"

"Who told you it was a doodle wall?"
the lady wants to know.

"Our teacher, **Mr Fullerman**. He said the council set
it up for kids like us to draw on."

"OH, REALLY?"

"**Yes** – it's on the leaflet," I explain.
"We're the first kids to arrive, which is
good news for me!"

"I see. So there'll be more kids turning up as well?"

"Probably. One kid in particular will be really
CROSS that we're here FIRST!"

The lady takes a photo of the doodles on the wall, then asks,

"Is there a parent or grown-up with you?"

"Yes, my dad's here. He drove us in that car. You can't miss it." I point it out.

"The one with the hot dog on top?" she asks.

"That's it."

"OK, stay there, will you? I just need to make a quick phone call. What's your name, by the way?"

"It's TOM. I've got lots more doodling to do, so I'll be here for a while," I say, and the lady goes off and leaves me to it.

(I particularly like the picture of Delia I've added.)

I'm <u>SO</u> busy drawing, I don't notice that
AMY, Derek and Norman have GONE.

"Hey, where is everyone?" I wonder, looking
round. Then Dad starts waving his arms at me.

"PPSSSSSSSSTTTTT, TOM!
Come over here quickly.
We need to GO!"

"But I haven't finished my doodle yet —
what's the hurry?" I ask.

"TOM! Get in the car.
Come along - NOW!"

"All right, Dad, I'm coming,"
I tell him, then pick up my pens
and go join them.

(I don't have a choice, really.)

Dad told us it was an EASY mistake to make and that LOADS of other kids would probably do exactly the same thing as we'd just done.

he keeps saying as we drive everyone home.

"Just checking – no one wrote their name on the wall, did they?" Dad asks.

"I might have done..." AMY says.

"Maybe I did too..." Norman adds.

"I wasn't going to ... but then I did," Derek tells us.

"I just wrote TOM. No one will know it's me, though. I don't think I drew a face."

"Mr Gates, are we in TROUBLE?" AMY asks my dad.

"No one's in any trouble, AMY," he tries to reassure us.

"Not yet, anyway," Derek whispers.

"That lady you were talking to didn't seem very happy, did she?" Norman points out.

"I didn't notice," I tell Norman while trying not to make things worse.

"What did she say to you, Tom?" Dad asks.

"Ummmm... She took a photo of the wall then told me she was going to make a phone call," I say, and from the way Dad **sighs** I think I might have said the wrong thing.

"A PHONE call?" Dad repeats.

"TO THE POLICE?" Derek shouts.

(Uh-oh. That doesn't sound good.)

"Don't worry, kids. It wasn't your fault. The council should have made it clearer on the leaflet," Dad tells us.

"And apart from that lady I don't think  anyone saw us," I add helpfully.

"It's not like we stand out much in this car, right?" Norman adds (not helpfully).

(S i l e n c e .)

"After I drop you all home I promise I'll go back and sort everything out. Anyone who sees the council leaflet will understand it was an EASY mistake to make. It should have been MUCH clearer..."

Council Doodle Wall is at **1 Drawing Road**

RIGHT HERE

(EASY TO MISS)

Trying NOT to worry about drawing on the **WRONG WALL** isn't easy, especially as Dad keeps driving past these signs.

NO DRAWING ON WALLS

DO NOT GRAFFITI

THAT MEANS YOU!

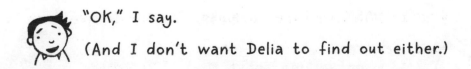

When we get home, Dad's keen to try and make things better. "I promise it will all be fine, Tom. I'll talk to your mum so you don't have to," he tells me.

"OK," I say.

(And I don't want Delia to find out either.)

Dad drives straight back to the WALL to sort things out while I go into the house. The first person I 'BUMP' into is Mum, who asks,

"Where's your dad gone now?"

I avoid the question and say,

   "Umm ... he said he won't be long."

"Yes, but where's he gone, Tom?" she wants to know. I'm trying NOT to say anything about drawing on the WRONG WALL when Delia turns up and starts BOTHERING me as well.

"Dad better not park that car outside our house. It's SO EMBARRASSING. That reminds me, Tom," she begins to say when I blurt out,

 "I DON'T KNOW WHERE DAD'S GONE!"

"I'm not asking about that..." Delia says.

(Oh.)

"Did you answer the DOOR when I asked you NOT to? I'm expecting someone important who hasn't turned up yet," she tells me.

"NO!" I say really quickly, because it's all coming back to me now (and not in a good way).

Give this to Delia.

"Are you SURE, Tom?"

Delia asks. Then Mum interrupts.

"Did your dad say how long he was going to be?"

And I start to get confused.

"Errr... He's not going to be long."

Then DELIA jumps in.

"You're HIDING something."

"NO I'M NOT."

"Yes you are - I can tell from your face."

"**W**hat about my face?"

"You know crossing your eyes and fingers doesn't work, don't you? And if the wind changes, you'll get stuck like that," Delia tells me.

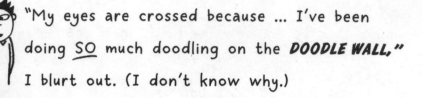

"My eyes are crossed because ... I've been doing <u>SO</u> much doodling on the **DOODLE WALL,**" I blurt out. (I don't know why.)

"How was that, Tom? Did you have a good time?" Mum asks.

"I did - I drew <u>LOTS</u> of weird **MONSTERS** and things all over the wall."

(I look over in Delia's direction just for fun.)

"You better <u>NOT</u> have drawn ME on that wall. You **KNOW** I'll find **OUT,**"

she says dramatically.

"**Ha!** You don't know where the wall is."
I LAUGH.

"I do, Tom. I've seen the leaflet.

The wall's on Drawing Road."

"That's **NOT** the wall we drew

on, though!" I tell Delia, then do a small

celebration dance. (A bit too early.)

What do you
mean, Tom?

Where did your dad
take you, then?

Uh-oh.
"To a wall, a nice **BIG** wall, that was..."

I try and explain until Delia interrupts me.

"You drew on the WRONG WALL, didn't you?"

"It was the RIGHT wall, just in

the WRONG place, that's all."

"Nice try, Tom."

"Thank you," I whisper, hoping Dad will come back soon and sort this all out.

"Did Dad take you to Drawing Road?" Mum asks.

"Nearly..." I say.

"When he gets home, I'll ask him EXACTLY where you went." Mum sighs. "Nothing's EASY in this family!"

"Tell me about it," Delia agrees and starts to head out of the room, when Mum tries to stop her.

"Hang on! While you're both here, I need to talk to you about your GRANDPARENTS' WEDDING! HAVE you both got something to wear?"

(S I L E N C E .)

"Clothes?" I say quietly.

"Funny..."

"You know what I mean, Tom. It would be nice for you both to wear something a little SMARTER. Try a DIFFERENT look for a change," Mum says.

"Like SMILING," I suggest, helpfully.

"My clothes are fine and I'm not wearing anything fancy," Delia says grumpily.

"All I'm saying is it's Bob and Mavis's special day and we should all make an EXTRA effort for them."

"I like the way I look and I'm not changing it for ANYONE," Delia tells us and stomps off.

"That's not what I meant at all!" Mum sighs. "You don't mind wearing something a little smarter, do you, Tom?" she asks me.

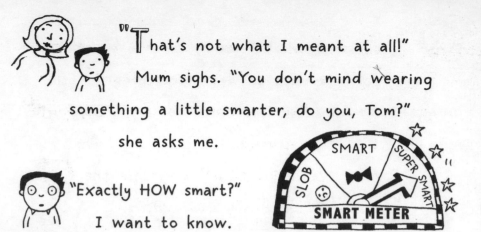

"Exactly HOW smart?" I want to know.

(I'm guessing SUPER SMART.)

SMART METER
SLOB   SMART   SUPER SMART

"At least I found my lovely old vintage dress for the party. I'd forgotten all about it."

"That's great, Mum," I say.

"It's gorgeous - real silk, too. Let me go and get it," Mum says. (I'm just glad she's stopped talking about me being smart.)

Mum shows me her dress, which she seems
pleased about. "I couldn't afford
something like this now," she says, *SWISHING*
the dress around.

"Isn't it a bit OLD?" I ask, as the
sleeves are puffy and odd.

"It's VINTAGE, Tom! That's a good thing!" She *LAUGHS*,
then adds, "Talking about all things VINTAGE, I'm
going to take the cake plate back to your granny's.
I won't be long." OK!

"While I'm gone you could do some drawing
for me to keep yourself busy? Make a
congratulations card for Granny and
Granddad!" Mum suggests.

"Yes! Good idea!" I say.

"And don't bother looking for any treats –
there aren't any."

"All right, Mum."

(She always hides the good snacks,
but I know where they are.)

73

"**T**here's NOTHING THERE!"

"Awwwwww."

Mum shouts, like she KNOWS what I'm doing. (How?)

Since I can't find ANY treats, I might as well start making a card for **THE FOSSILS**. I spread myself out across the whole kitchen table. It's NICE having it all to myself for a change. I start doodling some stars, a few hearts, a nice picture of me smiling. I use a **thick** black magic **marker**, which looks EXCELLENT.

There - all done.

I'm **VERY** pleased with my card ...

... until I pick it up and **NOTICE** my
doodle has gone **THROUGH** the paper
and right on to ...

... MUM'S VINTAGE DRESS. OH NO!

What am I going to do? I've **RUINED** her DRESS.

How am I going to fix it?

I'm trying to work out some kind of PLAN

when MUM comes back.

I *THROW* myself over her dress and cover it up with as much paper as I can. Then I try and ACT as relaxed as possible so Mum doesn't suspect a thing.

Gulp.

Hi, Tom!

"Hi, Mum! That was quick," I say.

"I know. Your granny tried to give me MORE cake to bring back, so I made my excuses to get home!" Mum LAUGHS. "And I wanted to try my dress on and check it still looks OK. I'm sure I left it here somewhere..." Mum says.

So I say, "I haven't seen it."

(And try to stay CALM.)

"There it is! Under your paper!" Mum says and picks her dress up and goes to LOOK in the MIRROR!

"NO, MUM, DON'T!"

I try and STOP HER.

"What's wrong, Tom?"

"Your dress looks ... so OLD," I blurt out.

"I didn't think it was THAT bad."

"You should wear something NEW, Mum. I think we should go SHOPPING," I quickly suggest.

"You want to go shopping? That's not like you, Tom."

"YES, I really do. In fact, I think we should go RIGHT NOW."

(I'll say anything to stop Mum seeing her DRESS.)

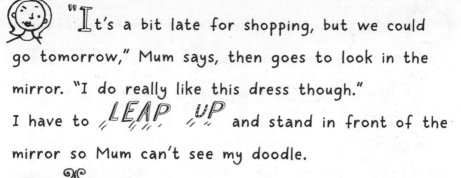

"It's a bit late for shopping, but we could go tomorrow," Mum says, then goes to look in the mirror. "I do really like this dress though."

I have to LEAP UP and stand in front of the mirror so Mum can't see my doodle.

"Tom, can you get out of the way? I can't see myself."

"But I just want to ...
GIVE YOU A BIG HUG."

"Awwwww, that's nice," Mum says, which gives me a chance to THINK THINK THINK to try and avoid

a DRESS DOODLE DISASTER.

(I could change the subject?)

For Delia.
Love letter?

"Delia's got a new boyfriend and I've met him.
He came to the house."

(It's all <u>kind of</u> TRUE.)

"Really? I wonder why she didn't tell us.
What's he like then, Tom?" Mum wants to know.

"I think he's in a band," I say.

"A musician?" Mum asks.

"A drummer." I nod, though I'm not entirely
<u>SURE</u> that's what he said. It seems to have worked
at DISTRACTING Mum from looking at her dress,
which is GOOD NEWS.

"Interesting... I might go and have a quick chat
with Delia, just to keep the lines of communication
open. You get yourself ready for bed, Tom,"
Mum tells me.

Result! "OK," I say, then NOTICE ...

... that Mum has left her dress behind. (YES!) THIS is my chance to HIDE it so she can't see the doodle. I've got so many things to remember!

① Make sure we don't get into trouble for the doodle wall.

② Fix Mum's dress.

③ Avoid Delia at all times.

④ Don't get any more sad faces at school.

It's a LOT. I head up to my bedroom and, after a quick look round, I decide to put Mum's dress in my WASH basket. (For now.)

Then I get my POSTER HOMEWORK (that I did EARLY) and put it NEXT to my pillow so it will be the FIRST THING I see 👀 when I wake up.

NEXT, I SPOT the envelope→ that bloke gave me for Delia. I can't give it to her NOW or she'll know I answered the door.

I'll sneak it into her room later when she's NOT there. I've been VERY busy... (No wonder I'm tired.)

BEEP BEEP BEEP

Huh?

Somehow I've managed to OVERSLEEP and now I'm going to be LATE for SCHOOL! (I <u>can't</u> get another SAD FACE. 🙁) So I brush my teeth in a *RUSH*, get dressed, eat breakfast and meet Derek as *QUICK* as I can. We do *FAST* WALKING all the way to school and we get there JUST in time for the bell. (Mr Fullerman hasn't started the register yet.)

We're not late! Hooray!

I tell Derek and run into class.

Marcus is already there. "Late again, Tom?"

He smiles.

"Not quite," I say

and sit down.

"Guess what?" he says.

"What?" I ask.

"**I** was the **FIRST** person at the *DOODLE WALL* and did the BEST drawing EVER. Where were you lot?" Marcus asks.

"We didn't go, Marcus. I was too busy doing my poster homework," I tell him.

Then **AMY** whispers to me, "Tom, did your dad sort everything out at the *DOODLE WALL?*"

But Marcus HEARS. "I thought you said you didn't go to the wall?"

"**W**e sort of went," I tell him.

"So **DID** you go or didn't you?" Marcus asks us both.

We did.

We didn't.

Make up your mind, then!

"We did go," **AMY** says. "Only we ended up drawing on the WRONG WALL. But it's OK as Tom's dad sorted everything out. None of us are in trouble, are we, Tom?"

"No, it wasn't our fault," I explain.

"SOUNDS like it **WAS** your fault to me. Looks like you **BOTH** might be getting one of these now."

Marcus has drawn a SAD FACE.

"I don't think so, Marcus," **AMY** tells him, then turns to me. "It was *FUN* doodling on the wall yesterday. Thanks for letting me copy your poster homework," she says.

"YOU COPIED TOM'S HOMEWORK?"

Marcus butts in.

"No. I did my own. We just doodled on the wall in Tom's style," **AMY** tells him.

"You doodled on the **WRONG** wall in Tom's style? Sounds like you'll be getting EVEN MORE SAD FACES if **Mr Fullerman** finds out."

"No one's going to be in trouble, Marcus," I say just before Mr Fullerman makes an announcement.

"MORNING, CLASS 5F! Can everyone take out their poster homework, please? I'm <u>really</u> looking forward to seeing them," he tells us.

I feel great about this as I've <u>done</u> my poster homework. 😊 I go to take it out and that's when I realize ... IT'S NOT THERE!

Where is it?!?

"Oh no..." I keep looking, but I've left it at home. "Not again, Tom," AMY whispers. "What are you going to do?"

"I don't know," I sigh.

"I do!" Marcus butts in again.

"It's four sad faces for you!

And we all know what FOUR sad faces means.

NO SCHOOL TRIP!"

This can't be happening.

Why do I always forget things? (Groan...)

Mr Fullerman comes over and tells the class,

"Hold your poster homework up so I can collect it, please."

Then AMY slides her homework over to me.

"Take it," she whispers.

"What?" I say, as I'm not sure what she's doing.
But before I can ask, Mr Fullerman IS STANDING
BEHIND ME ...

... and he picks it up.

"Thank you, Tom, I know you were looking forward to doing this homework for a change!"

he tells me then starts to READ it. (Uh-oh...)

"Tom..."

"Yes, sir?" I say.

 **"You know this homework is supposed to be all about you and all the things <u>you</u> like doing."**

"Yes, sir."

"So looking at your poster homework, it says your favourite subject is ..."

"Does it? Well, that's true. Maths is one of my favourite subjects, sir. I just don't talk about it much," I explain.

"Who doesn't like spelling, sir?" I smile.

"You don't," Marcus points out when he really doesn't need to.

"AND you have a passion for ... GYMNASTICS?"

"I do. It's the best!"

"I'm learning all kinds of interesting things about you today, Tom," Mr Fullerman says.

Then Marcus starts waving his homework around and pointing at me. "SIR! SIR! SIR!"

"HOLD ON, Marcus. All I can say, Tom, is it's a good job you <u>DID</u> have your homework, or I'd have given you another SAD FACE. Right – Amy, can I see your homework next, please?"

"Errr... I'm sorry, sir, I FORGOT it."

AMY just about manages to say the words. "I'll bring it in tomorrow," she adds. (This sends Marcus into a **FRENZY** of waving.)

"Mr Fullerman! Mr Fullerman!"

"One minute, Marcus. Oh dear, Amy, that's not like you. I will have to take away one of your smiley faces. It has to be the same for everyone,"

Mr Fullerman explains.

"I know, sir," AMY sighs.

"I've never lost a smiley face before," she says sadly. (Now I feel bad.)

But Marcus can hardly contain himself. **"SIR! SIR!"** he shouts, "that's Amy's homework, sir. I saw her pass it to Tom!"

"Seriously, Marcus. Can you just keep quiet?" AMY tells him.

"RIGHT – exactly whose homework is this, then?"

"Is this **YOUR** homework, Tom?"

"No, sir, it's **AMY's** homework," I tell him.

"**YES!** I KNEW I was right. No one EVER listens to me." Marcus jumps <u>up</u>.

"Everyone listens to you, Marcus," I say.

(It's hard not to.)

Mr Fullerman's heard enough.

"This has taken up FAR too much of our class time already, so here's what's going to happen. Amy, no more swapping homework – and you'll lose one smiley face.

Tom, bring in your poster homework tomorrow. Until you do, you'll have another sad face. Right – do you both understand?"

Yes, sir.

Yes, sir.

Ha! Ha!

 **AMY** turns to me and whispers, "You could have just said it was your homework, Tom!"

"I know. I'm sorry, **AMY**. I didn't mean to get you into trouble," I tell her.

"I can't BELIEVE I've lost a smiley face," she says.

"I know how you feel," I say sympathetically.

I don't. Marcus adds (not helping).

I don't think today can get any worse.

Mr Fullerman gathers up everybody's poster homework (apart from mine), and then makes an announcement to the WHOLE class.

"Would EVERYONE like to hear more about the SCHOOL TRIP?"

"The school trip you won't be coming on, Tom, with your FOUR sad faces..." Marcus whispers.

"I am going, you'll see," I tell him, then imagine different ways to STOP Marcus from going instead...

"A biscuit factory."

A WHAT?

Wow!

Yes!

"Did Mr Fullerman just say what I thought he said?"
I ask AMY.

"He did, Tom."

Marcus starts singing a song
to celebrate.
"I'm going to a F-A-C-T-O-R-Y, a biscuit FACTORY."

"Do you have to keep singing, Marcus?" I ask.
"I think I do! I'm going to a FACTORY, a
biscuit factory... I love a biscuit!"

(Marcus is SO annoying.)

I just HAVE to go on the school trip NOW! I'm going to make sure I do ALL these things and then everything is going to be fine.

1. Make sure Derek, AMY and Norman don't get into TROUBLE for the *DOODLE WALL.*

2. Fix Mum's dress (somehow.)

3. Avoid Delia at all times.

4. Don't get any more SAD FACES.

5. Bring in my poster homework, get rid of one of my sad faces and GO ON THE SCHOOL TRIP!

Mrs Mumble interrupts with a very **CRACKLY** announcement that's hard to understand.

"Quiet, please! Let's hear what Mrs Mumble is trying to tell us."

"Hello, Oakfield School.

I'd like to make an announcement

about the ～～ ～～ council Doodle wall.

(Uh-oh... This doesn't sound good.)

I'm not panicking yet, though.

"It's come to our attention that some children have been drawing on the wrong wall. The correct wall is in DRAWING WRONG ROAD and NOT DRAWING LANE. Please read the council leaflet carefully before you doodle. I repeat, the ROAD – that's DRAWING ROAD Thank you."

(Now I'm panicking.)

"Ooh, Tom and **AMY**. That sounds like you two could be in trouble. That's one sad face for **AMY** and **TEN** for you, Tom," Marcus enjoys telling us.

"Marcus, that's <u>NOT</u> going to happen," **AMY** snaps.

"There's a first time for everything." Marcus smiles.

"Ignore him, **AMY**. It wasn't our fault. We'll be fine." (If Dad sorts it out).

As the bell goes for break-time (which is a relief), **Mr Fullerman** says,**"Tom, Norman, Mr Keen wants to see BOTH of you in his office."**

"Really, sir?" I ask.

"Yes – off you go..." **Mr Fullerman** tells us.

Norman and I are in NO hurry to get there.

Derek is already waiting outside.

"Did you hear Mrs Mumble's announcement? Do you think we're in trouble?" he asks.

"Maybe?" I sigh.

"We could pretend not to know ANYTHING about it," Norman suggests.

"And say someone else signed OUR names on the wall?" Derek says.

"Did you write your name on the wall?" Norman asks me.

"Maybe a little," I sigh.

"Hey I've got an idea – how about I create a distraction by jumping around a lot – LIKE THIS," Norman says, then demonstrates for us.

"I'm not sure that's going to work, Norman," I tell him. "You jump really fast, though."

"Thanks!" Norman stops when Mr Keen opens his door and calls us in.

"Come in, you three. I need to speak to you urgently."

We follow Mr Keen into his office.

"Have you got any idea why you're here?" he asks us.

"Not really, sir," I say.

"I've heard that you've all been up to SOMETHING..." he tells us.

"Have we, sir?"

"I don't think so, sir," Derek says.

"Whatever it was, it WASN'T US, SIR!" Norman shouts.

"Well, that's not what I've been hearing. I want to know if it's true that you three ..."

Gulp...

"... are all STILL in a band?"

YES, SIR! WE ARE!

"That's great news, boys. Have you been practising?"

"A little bit, sir," Derek tells him.

"In-between snack breaks," Norman says.

"We do practise though, sir," I add.

"In that case, how do you feel about playing a song at the Open Day assembly? Something to impress the new parents and all the other important guests coming that day."

"WE'LL DO IT, SIR!" we all shout.

"DOGZOMBIES RULE!"

We all high-five.

"I'm glad you're SO enthusiastic. You'd be doing the school a huge favour too. The Recycled Orchestra were all set to play until their instruments got mistaken for a pile of rubbish and were accidentally ... recycled."

"That's terrible, sir. But lucky for us!" I say and  try not to sound too pleased.

"It's an important day for the school, so don't let me down,  **!"**

"We won't, sir!" Norman shouts as we leave his office.

Yes!

"PHEW! I thought he was going to ask about the **DOODLE WALL.** Now all **DOGZOMBIES** have to do is play brilliantly at the open day. I'll get rid of ALL of my 🙁 sad faces and then I can go on the SCHOOL TRIP!" I tell Derek and Norman.

(That's the plan, anyway.)

"We should have a band practice at mine after school. As there's not much time, we'll have to concentrate really hard on the <u>MOST</u> important thing."

"Like what band snacks to have," says Derek.

"Exactly," Norman and I agree.

I go and see who's around and find Dad in his shed, so I tell him the good news.

"Guess what, Dad? **Mr Keen** wants **DOGZOMBIES** to play at the school Open Day."

"Well done, Tom – that's great!"

"We thought he wanted to tell us off about the **DOODLE WALL**...

BUT you've fixed it, haven't you?" I ask Dad (just checking).

"Not exactly, Tom. I was on my way back to the wall when the car broke down, and by the time I got there it was dark and there was no one around to talk to," Dad explains. "But I'll go back later and find that lady and sort everything out. Don't worry about a THING, Tom," he tells me ...

... just as **M**um pops her head round the door. "Don't WORRY about what?" she asks.

"Nothing!" we both say.

(Mum still doesn't know about the *DOODLE WALL* mix-up.)

"REALLY? Come on, I can tell something's up."

"It's just that the car broke down, but it's fixed now."

"And...?"

"**DOGZOMBIES** are playing at the Open Day!"

"Fantastic! But make sure you bring in your homework tomorrow, Tom. You left it behind!"

"I **KNOW!** I won't forget it this time. **D**erek and **N**orman are coming round for a practice later, and Dad's supplying the biscuits."

"Am I?"

"Thanks, Dad!"

Then Mum asks us both a question. "I don't
suppose that either of you have seen my
VINTAGE dress? It's completely DISAPPEARED!"
"NO! I don't know where it is," I say, a bit too
quickly.

"It'll turn up – things always do." Dad tries to
reassure her.

"Well if it doesn't, we'll have to go
shopping after all, Tom," Mum tells me.
"YEAH, shopping! , I love shopping!"
I say. (Pretending to be keen might distract Mum
from the missing dress, because I <u>know</u> it's in the
wash basket in my room.)

"OK, Tom, hopefully..."
Mum starts to say when the doorbell goes.
DING
DONG   "Derek and Norman are here for
band practice. Better go,"
I say, then pinch a packet of
Dad's biscuits on the way out of the shed.

Norman and Derek are keen to get started. Derek helps himself to a pair of shades I have in my room. "Are these your sister's?" he asks.

"Yeah, but it's OK. She has LOADS more, she won't miss them," I tell Derek, then count the band in for our warm-up.

"After four. One, two, three, four..."

(Having a good ROCK STAR POSE is an important part of being in a band, especially if you don't have many songs.) Norman spots a copy of **ROCK WEEKLY** and holds it up next to Derek's face.

"Hey, Derek, you look like Slash from Guns N' Roses without the hat!" Norman says.

"Not for long!" I say and go and find Granddad's top hat, which Derek is happy to try on.

How do I look?

Derek wants to know.

"Like Willy Wonka!" Norman LAUGHs.

(It's TRUE!)

We all have a go at wearing it, then try to get back to our band practice ... after Norman asks me a question.

"Hey, Tom, did your dad sort everything out at the **DOODLE WALL** last night?"

"Um ... kind of. Don't worry, though – it'll all be fine. But right now we need to KEEP FOCUSED and not waste any more time. So let's make this very important decision..."

I tell Derek and Norman.

"Cheesy puffs or biscuits?"

"BOTH!" Norman says, which works for me.

While we're sharing out the snacks, Delia knocks

KNOCK KNOCK at my door.

TOM! I need to talk to you! she shouts.

"Uh-oh..."

"Pretend we're not here. She'll go away," I say.

I know you're there.
I'm coming in... (Delia is not going away.)

I tell Derek to take off the hat so she doesn't see

he's been wearing it and I ———THROW it

on to my bed just as Delia barges in and shouts,

Tom - have you got something for me? Mum said someone came round and YOU spoke to them.

I say nothing and offer her a

cheesy puff instead ...

Gulp.

... Which isn't what she wants to hear.

I don't want a cheesy puff.

Biscuit?

Tom, WHO did you talk to?

Your boyfriend! We had a really nice chat.

I don't have a boyfriend. What did you say to him?

Ummm ... let me think.

Tell me!

Oh yes! He was surprised to hear that **One Dimension** is your favourite band!

ARE YOU KIDDING ME?

You said **One Dimension** is my favourite band? TOM!

Maybe...

Just a little.

You had their posters on your walls!

" **THAT WAS YEARS AGO!** Thanks a lot, Tom. No wonder I didn't hear anything back. And STOP going into my room and taking my sunglasses!

I sit on my bed to keep out of Delia's way.

Are you sure you don't want a biscuit?

Delia storms over to Derek, who hands them over quickly, and then she STORMS out of my bedroom and **SLAMS** the door.

"She does like **One Dimension** really," I say.

"They're not the worst band in the world," Norman agrees.

Derek looks worried.

"Don't worry, Delia's always grumpy," I tell him.

"It's not Delia, it's you. I think you sat on the top hat," he says.

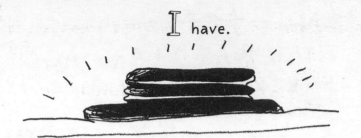

I have.

"OH NO! What am I going to do?"

"That looks really bad," Derek tells me.

"It's properly squashed," Norman adds.

"When's the wedding, Tom?" Derek checks.

"Maybe you can get a new one before then?"

"I can't get a **NEW** one - this hat's been in my family for years and years."

"You could say Rooster tried to eat it?" Derek suggests.

"Rooster does eat everything," I sigh.

"OR you could say a massive pigeon flew down, took the hat and ATTACKED it, like this..."

We watch Norman ACT out the whole scene.

(It's impressive.)

(OK – maybe not.)

"So what are you going to do, Tom?" Norman asks me.

(It's a good question.)

"When something like this happens, there's only one thing you can do," I say.

"Tell your mum and dad?" Derek asks.

"**NO**, hide it, of course."

I put the sᖠuᔕᕼᕮᑯ hat inside
my wash basket along with Mum's dress.

There, all done.

We finally get on and practise a few songs for the
school open day. So we are all ready to play <u>really</u> well.

I add Granddad's sᖠuᔕᕼᕮᑯ top hat to the list
of things that I have to SORT OUT. ☺

1)   Clean Mum's dress.

2)   Fix Granddad's top hat.

3)   Make sure my friends don't get into trouble
       about the ***DOODLE WALL.*** ☺

4)   Avoid Delia (unless I can FIND that envelope
       and slip it into her room like I had NOTHING
       to do with it).

5)   DON'T get any more SAD FACES at school. ⊗

6)   Remember to BRING <u>IN</u> my poster homework.

7)   Go on the school trip to

THE BISCUIT FACTORY.

(That's a lot of things.)

But it's OK because we've had an excellent band practice and I'm going to bed EARLY, so I am going to be BRIGHT and SPARKY for tomorrow.

I've also found a spare wafer, which is always a TREAT!

(And, of course, I brush my teeth.)

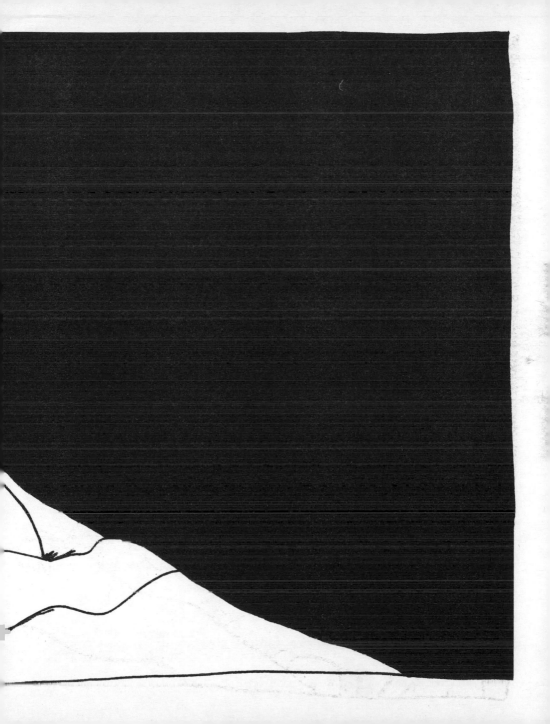

"TOM, YOU'RE LATE! HURRY UP!"

Oh no! What's the time? I can't be late today!

I need to be *SUPER═══SPEEDY.* I don't want ANOTHER SAD FACE. I get dressed FAST then run around my bedroom picking up everything I need – pens, paper, water bottle...

Phew, I almost forgot my HOMEWORK, but I **didn't.** :)

I shove it safely into my bag right next to my water bottle so I <u>know</u> where it is, grab breakfast, then *RUN* ═══════ all the way

to school.

Derek and **N**orman are there already.

So is **M**r **K**een, who looks pleased to see us.

"Morning, boys. Are you all set to play at the assembly this morning?" he asks.

"YES, SIR!" then **N**orman takes out his drumsticks.

"I've been practising my TWIRLING," he tells **M**r **K**een and nearly ((SPINS)) them out of his hands.

Mr **K**een steps back to a safe distance.

"Excellent! Let's show the new parents what a great school this is. Don't let me down, DOGZOMBIES !"

"YES, SIR!" we all say.

Mr **K**een goes off to talk to the people arriving. Then **D**erek suddenly *GASPS!*

"What's wrong?" I ask.

"Whatever you do – DON'T TURN AROUND!" he says.

... so we all turn around.

"OH NO! IT'S THE LADY FROM THE WALL!" I say.

"What's SHE doing here?" Derek wonders. (We all do.)

She's talking to Mr Keen.

"What if she tells him we drew on her wall?" Norman asks.

"She looks a bit cross," Derek tells us.

"Let's get to class then, before she sees us!" I suggest, but Derek wants to hear their conversation. He leans back casually and listens.

Mr Keen says, **"Welcome to our wonderful open day."**

"It's lovely to be invited," she replies.

"We've got a very impressive morning ahead, including a WONDERFUL school band who'll be playing for us."

"Uh-oh. That's us, time to go,"
Derek says, and we head off *quickly.*

**"They're KEEN to get to class,
I think. Let's join the others
and I'll show you around.
You're in for a TREAT today."**

"I'm really looking forward to it."

OAKFIELD SCHOOL OPEN DAY

We manage to get to class
without the lady seeing us.

"**T**om, please tell me your dad's sorted everything out with the you-know-what wall?"

is the first thing **AMY** wants to know when I sit down.

"Everything's going to be fine, although the lady from the wall is **HERE** in the school," I say.

"SHE'S **HERE?**"

"Yes, but she hasn't seen us, so DON'T worry."

"I'm not worried about ANYTHING," Marcus says.

"I don't have **FOUR** sad faces which means I'm going to a F-A-C-T-O-R-Y, A BISCUIT FACTORY!"

"Do you **HAVE** to sing, Marcus?" I sigh.

"I can't help myself, I'm just REALLY..."

"ANNOYING?" I say.

"No ... excited! Excited about seeing all the biscuits being made. It's going to be AMAZING.

Don't worry, Tom. I'll tell you all about it — as you're NOT going," Marcus tells me.

"I am going."

"Maybe, maybe not," Marcus says.

"Hey, Tom," **AMY** says, changing the subject, "are **DOGZOMBIES** playing in the school assembly?"

"YES! The plan is we'll be <u>SO</u> good that Mr Fullerman will take back ALL my sad faces ⊗ and he'll have to let me go to the **BISCUIT FACTORY** then." (I am being POSITIVE.)

"You'd better be good. You've got a LOT of sad faces to get rid of," ⊗ Marcus says.

 "We ARE good, and we're playing one of our BEST songs too."

"Is it as good as my song? You know, the one that goes I'm going to a F-A-C-T-O-R-Y, A BISCUIT FACTORY!"

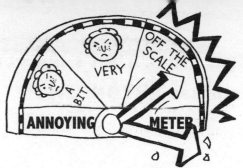

Mr Fullerman comes in and seems to be in a good mood. **"Morning, Class 5F. I hope you're all ready for the Open Day. And, Tom, have you got your POSTER homework with you?"**

"I have, Mr Fullerman. It's in my bag – I'll just get it."

"I've left a nice SPACE on the wall to pin it up."

"It's in here somewhere, sir..."

I am looking in my bag and I suddenly find my homework.

"OH NO! Sir, my water bottle must have leaked!"

"I've heard that one before..."

Marcus laughs.

"Oh dear, Tom. That's not going to impress ANYONE, is it?"

"No, sir."

"I can see that you at least TRIED to do your homework. So I'll give you one more chance. Go to the LIBRARY at break-time and do it again, OK?"

"Yes, sir!"

Marcus keeps singing in my ear.

"I'm going to a F-A-C-T-O-R-Y, A BISCUIT FACTORY!"

"I'll do it, sir!" I reassure him.

(I don't have a choice.)

I'll redo my homework, ✔ play amazingly well in **DOGZOMBIES**, ✔ avoid the lady from the wall, ✔ and EVERYTHING will work out **FINE**.

"Tom, Tom..." AMY says and starts shoving me.

"Look who's just walked into our class! It's the lady from the wall!"

"Oh no!"

We use our books to hide our faces. (I hope Norman hides as well!)

Uh-oh... ← He does

"Hello, Class 5F! We're just having a LOOK round the school, and I thought I'd show our guests some of the work you've been doing." Then Mr Keen tells the lady, "Mr Fullerman has been running a class achievement chart."

"That looks interesting," she says. "It helps to encourage the children to do their best," Mr Keen explains.

"Some people are doing better than others..."
Marcus mutters to me.

"Keep the books up and don't move," AMY tells me.
"They'll be gone soon."

"We just need to keep quiet and not attract any
attention at all," I agree with AMY.

"May I ask a question?" the lady asks.
"What do the children have to do to
get on the achievement chart?"

"Who'd like to answer that question?"
Mr Keen asks the class.

Marcus is DESPERATE to answer.

"SIR!
SIR!
I WILL!"

"**Go ahead, Marcus,**" Mr Fullerman says.

"You get a SAD  face for doing something wrong, like being LATE or forgetting your homework AGAIN."

"**Thank you, Marcus.**"

"And when you get FOUR sad faces, you WON'T be allowed on the SCHOOL TRIP."

"**Thank you, Marcus.**"

"AND you get a SMILEY 🙂 face when you do something right. BUT that hasn't happened for some people. AS YOU CAN SEE."

Marcus keeps looking at me.

I keep hiding behind my book.

Mr Keen interrupts Marcus. **"We do like the encourage children to take part in all kinds of activities. We'll be hearing a very special band in assembly later. Won't we, Mr Fullerman?"**

"You will, Mr Keen. Tom, Norman, raise your hands."

(I stay hidden and wave.)

 "We just get a bit nervous before we play," I try and explain. Me too...

"Excellent – we'll look forward to it. Thank you, Mr Fullerman. We're off to the school kitchens next where EVERYTHING is freshly prepared. We encourage HEALTHY EATING at Oakfield School. You won't find <u>FRIED</u> or FATTY foods here!"

"Do the kids feel like they miss out at all?"

the lady asks.

"NOT at all. It's something we're VERY proud of. You won't see chips on the menu at Oakfield School, THAT'S for sure," Mr Keen says and LAUGHs.

We breathe a sigh of relief when they go. "Finally..." I say to AMY, who points out something I hadn't thought of.

"So, Tom, your band is playing in front of EVERYONE and the lady will be there. How are you going to hide THEN?"

"I'll think of something."

I don't know what, though.

As I walk to the hall I have a bit more time to think. Mr Fullerman says Norman and I can get ready to play for the Open Day, so we meet Derek behind the school stage. Thanks to caretaker Stan, everything is set up and ready to go. BUT we still have a BIG problem to solve.

"Do you think she's told Mr Keen anything?" Derek asks.

"No, I don't think so," I say.

"Norman and I hid when she came into class, but she'll see us on stage," I say.

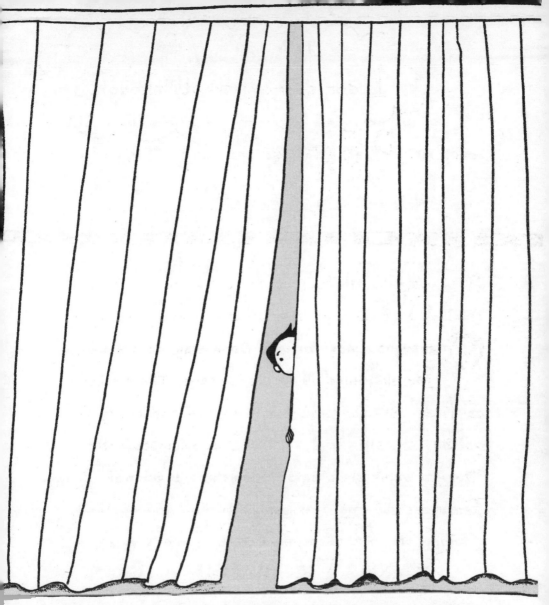

I have a sneaky peek from behind the curtain and
the LADY is SITTING in THE FRONT ROW! (Oh no...)

"I've got an idea," Norman says. "We could ALL keep moving really fast so she can't SEE our faces.

We'll be like a BLUR."

(Then Norman demonstrates.)

"I don't think that's going to work," Derek tells him.

"No, it won't, but maybe something ELSE will," I say and point to the dressing-up basket and costumes hanging up in the corner.

"Let's have a look, then," Derek says.

So we do.

Mr Keen begins the school assembly
as we get ready to play...

(Sort of.)

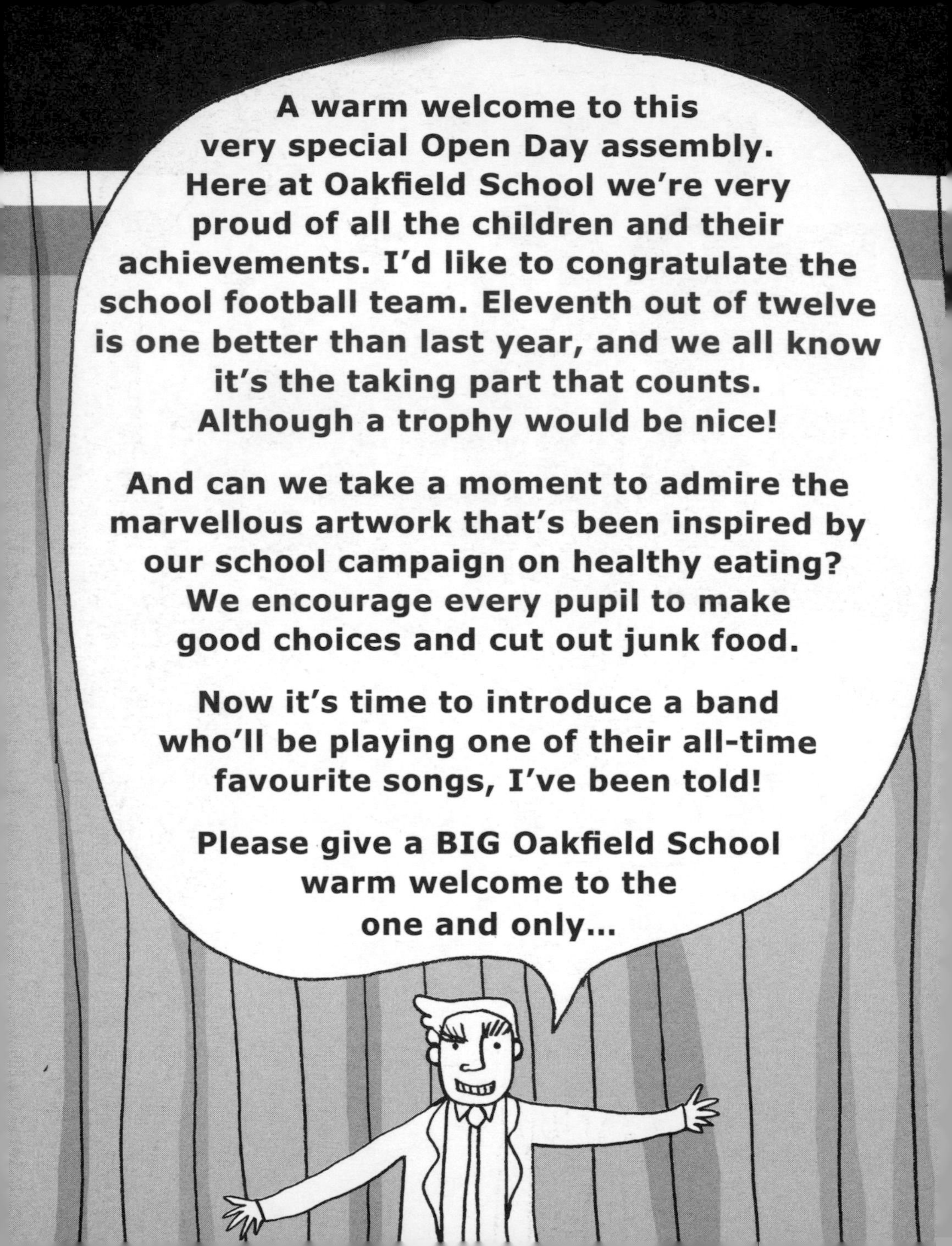
A warm welcome to this very special Open Day assembly. Here at Oakfield School we're very proud of all the children and their achievements. I'd like to congratulate the school football team. Eleventh out of twelve is one better than last year, and we all know it's the taking part that counts. Although a trophy would be nice!
And can we take a moment to admire the marvellous artwork that's been inspired by our school campaign on healthy eating? We encourage every pupil to make good choices and cut out junk food.
Now it's time to introduce a band who'll be playing one of their all-time favourite songs, I've been told!
Please give a BIG Oakfield School warm welcome to the one and only...

... and we've written
this song about
SCHOOL DINNERS.
It's called School Dinner Blues.
We hope you'll JOIN in and
sing along with us."

(I think our disguises are working.)

"Close your eyes and imagine
♫ While licking your lips
That today is the DAY
We'll be serving up

♫ ♫ CHIPS!

What do we want?

WE WANT CHIPS! ♪

When do we want them?

NOW!

♫

CHIPS! What do we want?

We want CHIPS!

When do we want them?

NOW!

CHIPS! CHIPS! CHIPS!

CHIPS! CHIPS! CHIPS!"

"No! No! No!"

We are in full flow when the sound goes off and
the curtains come down, so we're forced to STOP.

Ahem. There seems to be a slight technical problem and we've had to cut them short. I'd just like to point out that Oakfield School serves VERY healthy lunches every day.
No chips...
EVER.

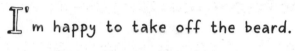I'm happy to take off the beard.

(It was scratchy.)

THE NEXT DAY

There's some GOOD NEWS and some BAD NEWS.

The GOOD NEWS is that, thanks to our excellent beard disguises, the lady from the wall didn't recognize us.

← Air punch

Mr Keen wasn't happy about our choice of song and was confused about the beards. But luckily EVERYONE else who heard our song **LOVED** it, so we didn't get into trouble for that. ✓ I EVEN remembered my POSTER homework too.

Mr Fullerman said, Well done, Tom! and took back one of my sad faces!

YES! ☺   BUT...

The BAD NEWS is:

I still can't go on the  SCHOOL TRIP.

Here's what happened:

I was in the library doing my homework when  Mr Keen brought the lady from the wall round. I dived under the table and bumped RIGHT INTO...

 BUSTER JONES, who was avoiding his detention.

He made me promise not to tell anyone where he was, and then said, "Go on, Gatesy, draw me a funny picture!" I couldn't say no to BUSTER JONES, so I drew a doodle I knew would make him laugh. Mr Fullerbum. Buster thought it was hilarious.

Ha! Ha!

But I'd only gone and drawn it on the BACK of my poster homework.

I didn't realize that until I handed it in to Mr Fullerman, who didn't think it was FUNNY at ALL.

Tom!

He gave me BACK my sad face. 🙁

Whoops.

You're running out of chances, Tom, Mr Fullerman told me sternly.

(So no school trip for me yet.)

And there's more BAD NEWS.

Granddad's hat is still squashed.

← I can't find the envelope that bloke gave me for Delia, who'll be even MORE furious if she finds out. So I'm avoiding her BIG TIME.

My doodles are also still all over Mum's vintage dress. And now Mum wants to go shopping because she can't find it anywhere.

I really didn't want to go shopping, BUT...

I overheard Delia on the phone telling Avril in a
really GRUMPY voice,

"No, nothing. Although I can tell Tom KNOWS
something. I'm going to find him and
ask him again."

I knew I had to act *FAST.*

So even though shopping was the LAST thing I
wanted to do, I found myself saying to Mum,

"YES, PLEASE, I'D LOVE TO COME!"

AND HERE
I AM. (Shopping.)

"Tom, what about this suit?
I like the colour. It's a
gorgeous shade of green,
don't you think?" Mum asks me.

"If you want to look like a Brussels sprout,"
I mumble. "Look! It's got a cute little
waistcoat as well," she points out, as <u>if</u>
that will make me change my mind.

"Do you want to try it on?" Mum smiles.

"Not really," I sigh.

"OK, we'll keep looking. I'm glad I've found a nice
dress for the wedding just in case my vintage
dress doesn't turn up. I <u>WISH</u> I knew where it
disappeared to. It's a real mystery," Mum says.

Not to me,
it's not.

I pick out something that
I like and hold it up.

"**W**hat about this T-shirt? IT'S PERFECT!"

I try and convince Mum.

"You're going to a wedding, not a concert, Tom. Let's find something a little more special," Mum tells me and picks out another suit that's even WORSE than the last one.

"Mum, I'm not wearing a suit!" I say and I'm just about to look for something else when I suddenly spot the LADY FROM THE WALL! And she's only walking towards me. What's she doing here?

This is a disaster!

I grab the suit from Mum and loads of other RANDOM clothes too, then shout, "I've changed my mind! I LOVE it. I want to try EVERYTHING ON RIGHT NOW.

Here I go!"

"OK, Tom, I'll wait outside the changing room for you. Well done!"

I disappear as quickly as I can – and just in time, as the lady is only right OUTSIDE and she starts talking to MUM!

"Do you mind me asking where you found that dress?" I hear her say.

WHAT AM I GOING TO DO NOW?

"On that rail behind you. It's lovely, isn't it?"

"That's just what I'm looking for, thank you," the lady tells Mum.

(Phew. She's going to LEAVE and everything will be fine...)

"I think I'll try it on," the lady adds.

"My son's in the changing room, but he won't be long. Tom, are you ready? Hurry up!"

Come on, TOM!

This lady is waiting!

OH NO!

I can't let her see me.

I put on ALL the clothes at
the same time and hope for
the best as I emerge from
the changing room – slowly.

"What are you wearing, Tom?
It's a wedding, not a fancy dress party!" Mum tells
me as I try to HIDE my face.
(So far the lady doesn't seem to recognize me.)

"Where's the suit, Tom?" Mum asks.

"Underneath," I mumble.

"Come on, let me see it." Then she tries to take

off my coat, while apologizing to the lady, who asks,

"Do you mind if I try the dress on now?"

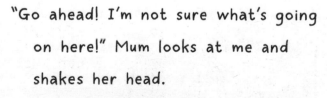

"Go ahead! I'm not sure what's going
on here!" Mum looks at me and
shakes her head.
(I keep quiet.)

Mum takes off the **BIG** coat to see the suit.

"Oh, that looks great, Tom.

But maybe without the hat?"

I can't waste any time so I say...

"LET'S BUY IT

NOW, I LOVE THIS SUIT.

We can pay over there."

(I'm trying to leave the shop

before the lady comes out of the changing room.)

"You need to change back into your own

clothes first," Mum tells me.

"No I don't, Mum. **PLEASE** can I wear the

suit **RIGHT NOW?** It's the **BEST** and

I don't want to take it off."

"All right, Tom, but don't get it dirty.

I'll get your clothes. Hang on,

I just want a quick photo..."

"MUM! Do you have to?"

"You look SO smart, though!" she tells me. I don't make a fuss.

Instead, I run to the counter to avoid the lady and Mum follows me.

"Isn't that your friend Marcus waving at you?" she asks.

(Why did it have to be Marcus?)

"Aren't you going to wave back?"

I give him a small wave because I know Marcus will be EXTRA annoying in school now. Then Mum pays for the suit and we make it out of the shop before the lady sees me.

PHEW...

Mum keeps taking sneaky pictures of me all the way home. "I'll send them to your grandparents," she tells me – like THAT makes it better.

▪▪▪▪▪▪▪▪▪▪▪▪▪▪▪▪▪▪▪▪▪▪▪▪▪▪▪▪

Someone else that I don't want to BUMP into when I get back to the house is Delia. (She'll just LAUGH at me and start asking more questions.) I almost make it up to my room when I see Dad.

"TOM! Nice suit!"

"Thanks, Dad. Did you sort things out at the wall like you said you were going to?" I want to know.

"Not yet, Tom, but I will. Don't worry about a thing!" he tells me.

Mum overhears us talking.

"**W**ho's worried about what?"

"**NOTHING!**" I shout a bit too loudly.

"Tom, don't get the suit dirty. You need to take it off, remember?" she tells me. "Which reminds me, where's your washing?"

"I've got some to do as well, so I'll grab Tom's," Dad says and I start to panic as I remember

WHAT'S IN MY WASH BASKET!

"**DON'T GO IN MY ROOM!**"

I yell.

"All right, Tom," Dad says.

"It's just I've got a surprise for you and I don't want you to see it. <u>I'll</u> bring my own washing down," I tell them both (and smile).

"Fine, Tom - but take the suit off, will you?" Mum reminds me again.

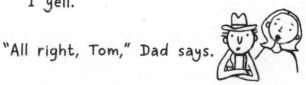

As I'm about to disappear into my room, Dad asks,
"I don't suppose you've seen Granddad's top hat,
have you, Tom?"

"Is that missing too? I still can't find my vintage
dress," Mum adds.

 I try and act as normal as possible and say,
"I don't know where anything is," then
escape to my room.

What am I going to do? If Mum and Dad see I've
got the hat and the dress, I'll be in trouble and
they might NOT let me go on the school trip.

Don't forget to bring your washing down!

Dad shouts through my door,
which gives me an idea.

"**W**hy didn't I think of this before?

I'll put the dress in the washing machine! I mean, how hard can it be to wash a dress?

(I'll put the hat under my bed for now.)

Sneaking down to the washing machine is the EASY BIT.

Trying to work out what to do next isn't so simple.

There's a **lot** of different washing stuff to use.

I shove in Mum's dress, then add a bit of EVERYTHING. Some powder, two of these, maybe a bit of this, another one of those.

Washing tablets

POWDER

That should get the doodles out of Mum's dress.

(One more for luck.)

All I have to do is TURN the machine on.

I'm deciding which buttons to press when

I can hear someone walking down the corridor...

So I HIDE JUST IN TIME. IT'S DELIA! She piles her own clothes into the machine, adds MORE powder and turns it on. ☺

Which is a RESULT as Delia's done it ALL for me.

THIS IS EXCELLENT! I wait until she leaves then sneak back to my room, take off the suit, then go down to the front room and lie on the sofa for a nice RELAXING time. I'm busy reading a COMIC when

THE FOSSILS come over to say, "Hello!"

"We were just passing through and wanted to check the top hat still fits," Granddad announces.

"Do you think you could get it for me, Tom?"

(Uh-oh...)

I jump up. "I can't, Granddad."

"Why's that, Tom?" Granny wonders.

"Because ... it's not here. It's ... being washed for the wedding!"

"Washed?" Granddad repeats.

"Yes, washed – cleaned."

"That's a good idea. You want to look your best, don't you, Bob?"
Granny asks him.

"I suppose everyone will be looking at me," Granddad says and Granny gives him a LOOK.
(I'm hoping they won't ask any more questions about his top hat.)

"All we want is for everyone to have a FUN and relaxed day," Granny tells me.

"But not SO relaxed that Teacup Tony falls asleep." Granddad LAUGHs.

"Are **Teacup Tony and the Saucers** playing at the wedding?" I ask.

 "I hope so! But Teacup Tony might need a little power nap to keep him going," Granny tells us.

 "He might not be the only one!" Granddad winks at Granny.

"You'll be fine, Bob," Granny tells him.

"I wasn't talking about me," he jokes.

"Very FUNNY, Bob. The party's at the LEAFY GREEN OLD FOLKS' HOME, so I hope it's not going to be..."

"RUINED!"

Mum storms in and shouts, "LOOK! Delia put my silk dress into the washing machine with all of her **BLACK** clothes!"

 "Oh no, that's terrible. What was she thinking?" I say.

"I bet she just *THREW* it in without even reading the washing label!" Mum tells us.

"YES, that's EXACTLY what she did." I nod.

"It's all GREY and ripped." Mum sighs.

"A bit like ME!" Granddad jokes.

 (Mum ignores him.)

"Oh, that's such a shame, Rita. I'm sure Delia didn't mean to ruin your dress."

"Is Delia going to be in trouble?" I ask.

"I don't know, Tom. I'll have to ask her what happened. How can I wear this NOW?" Mum says.

"Oh, I don't know, Rita. There's a little touch of SHABBY CHIC about it, don't you think?" Granny tells Mum, but she's not convinced.

"It's more SHABBY than CHIC, Mavis. It would be fine if you were having a **HALLOWEEN** party and not a wedding."

"You could always wear the NEW dress you bought," I suggest. "Can I just check - it's still Delia's fault, right?"

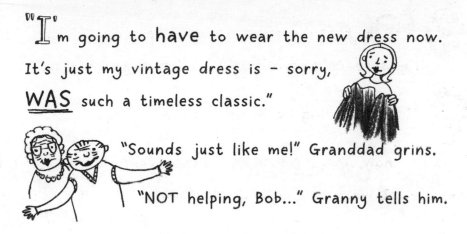

"I'm going to **have** to wear the new dress now. It's just my vintage dress is – sorry, <u>WAS</u> such a timeless classic."

"Sounds just like me!" Granddad grins.

"NOT helping, Bob..." Granny tells him.

"I think I'll go and have a chat with Delia – find out if she did this, and what ELSE is going on in her life," Mum tells us and goes off to find her.

(I keep quiet.)

Then Granny tries to LIGHTEN the mood and says, "Well, the lovely thing about weddings is that they always bring EVERYONE together!"

"I'm **SO** looking forward to us all being **ONE BIG HAPPY FAMILY,**"

Granny says, just as Delia shouts from her room.

ARE YOU SERIOUS? NO, it wasn't ME who put your dress in the machine!

BANG!

"Well, that went well..." Mum says when she comes back.

"And THAT'S why we should really get a DOG!" I suggest.

"Nice try, Tom..." (It was worth a go.)

"Maybe your dad can talk to her, though I don't know where he's gone."

"**D**id he tell you where he was going, Tom?" Mum asks me.

"Ummm... not really," I say. "Better go and do my homework..." I add as an excuse to get back to my room. I really hope Dad <u>IS</u> at the wall and sorting everything out so I'll be able to go into school tomorrow and tell my friends that everything's FINE. 😊

Meanwhile, at the wall.

I can explain, officer. It was my son.

I'm painting over his doodles.

Really, sir? Blaming it on your own son?

You can come to the station and answer a few questions...

But I can't!

Oh yes you can, sir...

DRAWIN

Dad's in trouble.

Nᴇxᴛ DAY IN SCHOOL

I make a special effort to be on time as I don't want any more SAD FACES. 🙁

As soon as I sit down, Marcus says,

"I saw you the other day, Tom."

"Did you, Marcus? That must have been exciting for you."

"Not really, you were wearing a funny suit."

"It wasn't that funny," I sigh.

"It was," he insists.

"What's wrong with wearing a suit?" **AMY** asks Marcus.

"You didn't see the COLOUR of it." Marcus laughs.

"Shall we talk about something else?" I say, trying to change the subject.

"OK. Let's count how many SAD FACES 😞 we've all got on the achievement chart then. I've got one and LOOK, you've still got FOUR, Tom," Marcus says. 😞 😞 😞 😞

"You don't have to rub it in, Marcus."

"I'm just counting them, that's all. AMY still hasn't got any, have you, AMY?"

"No, Marcus." Then AMY turns to me.
"Don't worry, Tom. I managed to get my smiley face back," she says.

"How did you do that?" I ask.

"I did my poetry homework early."

"POETRY homework ...

 ... WHAT POETRY homework?"

"Not again, Tom! You'll never be able to come on the school trip if you keep forgetting things all the time."
AMY shakes her head.

"It's not looking good for the biscuit factory NOW, is it, Tom?" Marcus says.

How did I miss the poetry homework? What was I doing?

Don't forget to do your poetry homework

Me doodling

"Morning, Class 5F. I'm really looking forward to hearing your poems! And I've got more NEWS on the school TRIP to the biscuit factory, so LISTEN carefully."

"You don't have to listen, Tom," Marcus tells me smugly.

"I AM still going," I say.

"We'll see," Marcus adds.

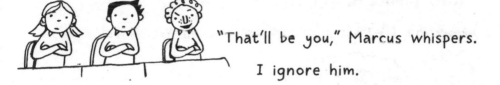

"If you're coming on the school trip, I need your signed permission slips back by tomorrow at the very latest. And anyone who's NOT joining us ..."

"That'll be you," Marcus whispers.

I ignore him.

"... will be spending some quality time with Mrs Worthington for a double maths class instead."

"Well, I know where I would rather be..."

Marcus smiles.

"Marcus! As you seem to be so interested in sad faces, would you like me to add one to your chart?"

"No, sir."

 "Right then. It's time to hear your homework. Tom, would you like to go first? It's never too late to gain back a smiley FACE." 🙂 Mr Fullerman is trying to be nice, but I <u>don't</u> HAVE any poetry homework, so I stall for time.

"One minute, sir. It's just in my bag..."

I have a good rummage around and find ... the ENVELOPE that bloke gave me for Delia. Which is not what I want right NOW.

"Is that it, Tom?"

"No, sir – I'm still looking," I say quickly. Then I spot a caramel wafer wrapper in the corner of my bag and that gives me an IDEA.

"You do HAVE a poem, don't you, Tom?"

"I'VE DONE MINE, SIR!" Marcus shouts.

"Sir! I've got it, but I need **N**orman to come and help me," I say. **N**orman looks confused.

Huh?

"What, me?" he checks.

"Yes! Remember the song we practised the other day? It's sort of a poem," I explain and we have a quick practice first.

"Ready, sir!

This is called ...

The Biscuit Song!"

(The class starts laughing.)

Ha! Ha! Ha! Ha! Ha! Ha!

"Settle down, Class 5F. Ready when you are, boys We haven't got all day,"

Mr Fullerman says.

"They're making it up, I can tell," Marcus says.

"Stop being a twit, Marcus!"

AMY shuts him up as we're about to start.

"It's about our FAVOURITE biscuits, and NOT about FIG ROLLS - nobody likes those,"

I announce.

"I quite like them, but let's get on with the poem, shall we?"

Mr Fullerman tells us. So we do.

174

The Biscuit Song!

"Biscuits here, biscuits there,
Eat a biscuit everywhere,
Crunchy biscuits, custard creams,
Biscuits in your biscuit dreams.

"Shortbread biscuits, ginger nuts,
Jammy biscuits pick you up,
Chocolate cookies, chocolate chips,
Melted chocolate on your lips.

"Say YEAH! YEAH! Move your biscuit feet.
Say YEAH! YEAH! To the biscuit beat.
Say YEAH! YEAH! It's a biscuit treat,
Biscuits plain and biscuits sweet!"

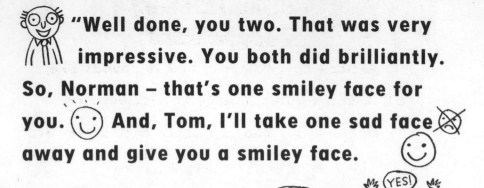

"Well done, you two. That was very impressive. You both did brilliantly. So, Norman – that's one smiley face for you. :) And, Tom, I'll take one sad face away and give you a smiley face.

"Does that mean I can come YES! on the school trip after all, sir?"

YES!

I ask.

"It does, Tom. Keep up the good work."

I sit back down and start singing...

"I'm going to a FACTORY, a BISCUIT FACTORY!"

"Well done, Tom, that was GREAT!" AMY smiles.

"It was OK ... if you like biscuits," Marcus grumbles.

(I do!)

Now I can tell Mum and Dad about the school TRIP!

Back at HOME

I'm excited to get home, and it sounds like everyone's in the kitchen. I have to risk bumping into Delia as Mum and Dad are there too. I run into the kitchen only to hear Mum say,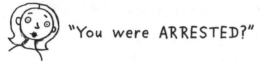

"You were ARRESTED?"

"Rita, it's not as bad as it sounds. Just a small misunderstanding, that's all," Dad explains. Delia is shaking her head in a disapproving way.

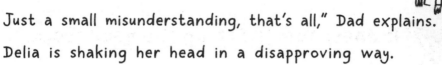"What exactly were you arrested for?"
Mum wants to know.

"Crimes against fashion? Bad taste in music? Take your pick," Delia says.

"Thanks for that, Delia. Actually, what happened was I ACCIDENTALLY took the kids to the WRONG

DOODLE WALL. Which was really the council's fault for not making it clear on the leaflet..."

177

"So I went back to paint it over, and that's when I got arrested."

"Tom better not have drawn a picture of ME on that wall," Delia says, right in front of me.

"I am here, you know,"

I remind her, then WISH I hadn't.

"Well DID you?" she asks again.

"Errr ... I don't remember."

"If it was the council's fault, why did they arrest you?"

"Someone must have reported me when I was painting over the doodles. But once I showed them the leaflet at the station, it was fine. I don't think I'll be going to prison." Dad LAUGHs.

(Which is good to know.)

This seems like a good time to SHARE my news.

"Guess where I'm going on the SCHOOL TRIP!"

"A museum?" Mum wonders.

"NO, I'm going to a
BISCUIT FACTORY!
TOMORROW!"

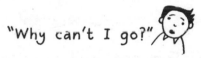

I shout in a very excited way.

 "Shame you can't go, though, isn't it?"
Delia adds and I'm not expecting her
to say that.

"Why can't I go?"

"Because our grandparents are getting remarried, or
had you all forgotten? I'm guessing YES."
Delia is looking at us and shaking her head again.

"NOOOOOOOOOOO! It can't be!"
I'm shocked, and so are Mum and Dad.

"Are you sure about that, Delia?"
Mum says, trying to remember the date.

Delia keeps us waiting before saying...
"IT'S A JOKE. It's not tomorrow – it's the
day after, of course. Your faces..."
She's almost smiling.

Then Mum says, "Honestly, Delia, you gave me
a shock. I've still got so much to do."

"I haven't got my suit ready and we need to give
Bob his TOP HAT," Dad adds while I'm
thinking ... no we don't – not unless he wants
to wear it all squashed.

"Speaking of the TOP HAT, I can't find it
anywhere. Has anyone seen it?" Dad asks us.

"Did anyone give it to Bob already?"
Mum wonders.

"I don't have Granddad's hat,"
Delia tells us.

(I keep quiet.)

Instead I bring out my permission slip to get signed.
"It's for the **BISCUIT FACTORY** trip.
I CAN'T FORGET IT or I won't be
allowed to go and I'll have to stay with
Mrs Worthington, which would be the WORST."

"I'd feel sorry for Mrs Worthington,"
Delia tells me.
(She is FULL of jokes today.)

Very funny.

I tell everyone, "This school trip is going to be
BRILLIANT! There'll be LOADS of BISCUITS
everywhere! And I'll even get to see CARAMEL
WAFERS being made too!"

I'm so excited, it's going to be hard to get to sleep...

I'm still **THINKING** about the
BISCUIT FACTORY
when I go to bed.

This is going to be the most

sPEcTAcuLAR
scHOOL TRIP
EvER!

When we all get to the **BISCUIT FACTORY,** it's not exactly how I imagined.

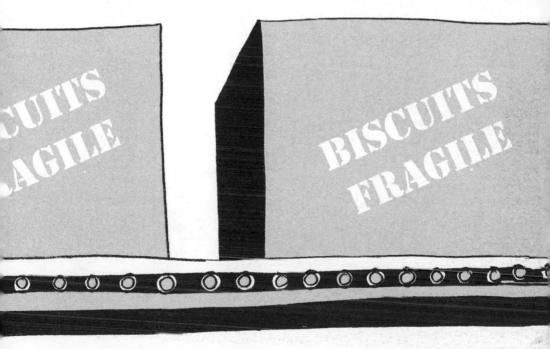

BISCUITS FRAGILE

The hair nets were a surprise...

"The ingredients are then carefully mixed for ten minutes and forty-two seconds exactly," the tour guide tells us.

AMY puts up her hand. "Excuse me, we can't actually SEE anything."

(Good point, AMY.)

"That's right. It's <u>all</u> sealed in to avoid any contamination, as every biscuit has to taste the same," she explains, not making it sound very exciting at all.

"Isn't that interesting, children?"

Mr Fullerman asks enthusiastically.

(S I L E N C E .)

"Does anyone have any questions?"

our guide wonders.

"I do. When do we get to eat some biscuits?" Norman wants to know.

(It's an excellent question.)

"There are biscuits being made FRESH today that will be available to taste at the end of the tour."

We all do high-fives.

"What biscuits are you making today?" AMY asks.

"We produce a variety of biscuits in the factory and today we're making some of our very best sellers."

"CARAMEL WAFERS?" I call out.

"Fig rolls."

"Oh." I sigh.

(That's not what we wanted to hear.)

"Come on, you lot. Who doesn't love a fig roll?" Mr Fullerman asks us all.

(All our hands go up.)

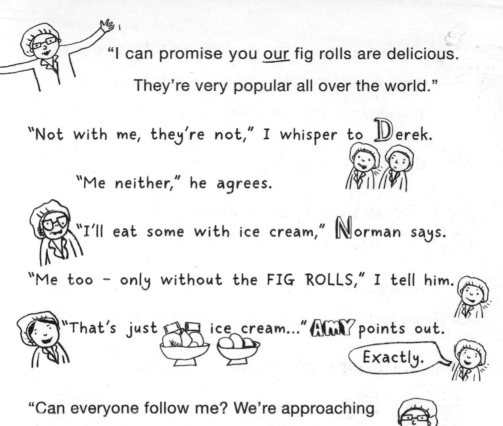

"I can promise you <u>our</u> fig rolls are delicious.
They're very popular all over the world."

"Not with me, they're not," I whisper to Derek.

"Me neither," he agrees.

"I'll eat some with ice cream," Norman says.

"Me too - only without the FIG ROLLS," I tell him.

"That's just ice cream..." AMY points out.

Exactly.

"Can everyone follow me? We're approaching the area where the figs are gontly squeezed into the rolls. It's a complicated but **THRILLING** process as you can see. Please don't touch anything," our guide tells us STERNLY.

"What's over there?" Marcus asks, pointing to another room that's filled with equipment.

"Good question," our guide replies. "We work on NEW recipes in there, and right now we're busy developing a range of HEALTHIER biscuits for today's market that contain LESS sugar, LESS fat, and very little..."

Flavour? Derek adds, and the guide gives him a LOOK.

 "I was going to say, VERY little in them that isn't completely natural."

"That's great. Shall we get going?" Mr Fullerman suggests.

"Yes, I know the owner of the factory is very keen to come and say hello and meet you ALL."

"We'd love that, wouldn't we, children?"

"Is THAT when we get to EAT some biscuits?" Norman shouts out.

"I believe that's correct. This way, please. Mind your step," the guide says and we all follow after her.

"I wasn't expecting the factory to be like THIS, were you?" I say to Derek.

"No, I wasn't," he whispers as the tour continues.

"And THIS is where the biscuits are packaged and put into boxes then sent to shops for people everywhere to enjoy."

"Apart from us," I sigh.

"Thank you. That was, fascinating, wasn't it, children...?"

(S I L E N C E .)

"Yes, Mr Fullerman," we reply ... eventually.

 "Although our actual tour is over, I'd like you to meet the person who organized your trip. She can also tell you anything you want to know about this factory AND its biscuits." Our guide points to a lady holding a plate of biscuits. She is wearing the same outfit as us, AND a face mask, too.

"ARE THOSE OUR BISCUITS?"

Norman asks, very excitedly.

"Yes! I hope you enjoyed the tour?" the owner asks.

We are all slightly more enthusiastic now and do a little cheer.

"YEAH!"

"One of the reasons I was so keen to invite your school here was for the LAUNCH of our NEW biscuit. I'm guessing everyone here likes biscuits, right?"

"I LOVE biscuits the MOST!" Marcus shouts.

"And I also think that there might be some children here today who like doodling too. Is that right, Mr Fullerman?"

"That's true, I do have a very creative class."

 "I like doodling AND biscuits!" Marcus yells again.

"Hang on, let me take off this mask to talk to you properly," she says.

The last person I'm expecting to see is...

THE LADY FROM THE WALL!

"That's better, you can all hear me properly now," she tells us.

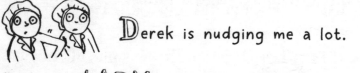 Derek is nudging me a lot.

"It's the LADY who saw us doodle on the wall, Tom," Derek whispers, still nudging me.

"OH NO!" I say, and we both try and hide.

AMY is just as surprised as we are.

 "It's the lady from the wall. Don't panic!" she adds. (Too late for that.)

"I wanted to find the person who DREW some doodles on my wall..." the lady announces.

Uh-oh ... what am I going to do now?

(I'm panicking.)

"It wasn't our fault, Tom," Derek says.

"Keep CALM, Tom," AMY adds and we all try and hide behind Solid.

"I took these photos of the wall BEFORE someone painted over it. Does anyone recognize them?"

I DO.

I'm trying to THINK,

when Marcus starts POINTING at ME.

"I know who did THEM! Those look like TOM'S doodles," he tells the lady.

"He's over there..."

"Are you Tom, then?" the lady asks.

I can't keep hiding behind Solid, so I start to slowly step forward, when Derek pushes in front of me and says,

"It's me. I'm Tom. I did those doodles.

None of us drew on your wall on purpose – honestly, miss..."

"It's Miss WAFER.

I'm the owner of the **BISCUIT FACTORY.**"

"Are you the <u>REAL</u> KAREN WAFER?" AMY asks.

(We all gasp as she's properly WELL known.)

"My whole name is KAREN M WAFER.

I'm sure you can work it out."*

"Miss WAFER, we didn't deliberately draw on your wall.

My dad got the address mixed up.

We meant to go to the council

DOODLE WALL."

I carry on trying to EXPLAIN what happened.

*Sounds like caramel wafer.

Marcus puts his hand up (again...).
"I want to point out that I drew on the RIGHT
wall," he tells us smugly.

(Typical Marcus.)

"ANYWAY." (I carry on talking.)

"We all copied my poster homework and then
I told everyone to write their names on the wall
because their doodles were SO GOOD.
So it's really my fault, not theirs,"

Thanks, Tom

my friends say. The lady puts
down her plate of biscuits
and takes out her phone and
shows it to me.

"So, can I be clear, these are your doodles,
Tom – is that right?"

"Yes, they're mine."

"Well, I have to say..." she says, then pauses...

"I LOVE them! They are really FANTASTIC. Especially the FREAKY monster with the sunglasses," the lady tells me.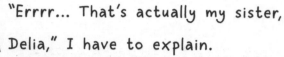

 "Errrr... That's actually my sister, Delia," I have to explain.

"I'm just glad I took a picture before your dad painted over most of the wall!"

 "Did he?"

"Almost. So listen, Tom, we'd like to use your style of doodles for the BRAND NEW biscuits we're making."

 "REALLY?"

I'm in **SHOCK.**

I wasn't expecting THAT!

"We'll talk to your parents, obviously. But your artwork will be on all the packets. I'd also like to donate some art equipment to your school. How does that sound?"

 "I THINK THAT SOUNDS GREAT, DOESN'T IT, TOM?" Mr Fullerman says.

"Wow. Does that mean my doodles will be on the NEW BISCUIT posters too?" I ask.

"That's right, Tom," Miss Wafer tells me.

"That's FANTASTIC!"
I say and everyone celebrates with me.
Even Marcus joins in.
"I'm pleased for you, Tom," he says, which
is almost nice of him.

Miss WAFER gives us some biscuits to taste, and we get to take some home with us too.

I discover that fig rolls aren't as bad as I thought they were.

But I leave most on a plate in the kitchen for everyone to help themselves, because I am a nice person 😊

(and I've had enough fig rolls for a while).

1970 ♥ ♥ ♥ 1970

Shoulder pads are in!

Jump back in time!

You are invited to the wedding of

Mavis Ethel Gates and Robert Edward

Gates, who are renewing their vows at:

THE LEAFY GREEN OLD FOLKS' HOME

The theme is 1970s DISCO.

Come ready to dance!

♡

The Fossils are having a **1970s** themed wedding, so Mum and Dad let me doodle on my 'SUIT' as it fits with the style. I don't mind wearing it now!

They were both **surprised** and pleased to hear my doodles were being used for the BISCUIT posters. Even Delia said well done.
(I kept quiet about drawing her on the wall.)

I didn't tell her I found the envelope the bloke gave me. I just snuck into her room and hid it under a pile of **ROCK WEEKLY**s.
Hopefully she won't know it was ME.
(Fingers crossed.)

I decided **NOT** to look inside the envelope in case it was some kind of love letter.

Yuck.

Granny and Granddad's Wedding
(again)

My suit ↓

It's Granny and Granddad's wedding day and I **SHOULD** be looking forward to it. BUT, there's a problem.

Granddad's hat still looks like THIS.

→ SQUASHED!

I can't fix it now.

I'll have to hand it over like that.

"HURRY UP, TOM, WE'RE ALL WAITING TO GO!"

Delia shouts at me through the door.

"I'M COMING!" I shout back, then
I hide the hat behind my back before going out.

"Nice suit, Tom," Delia says.

"Thanks, and you look ... EXACTLY the same."

"Did <u>YOU</u> leave that envelope in my room?"
she asks me, which is awkward.

"That depends..." I say.

"On what?"

"Whether you're cross with me."

"I WAS cross. But as it's Granny and
Granddad's wedding, I've made an effort to get
over it," she tells me.

"Sorry – it got lost in my room," I explain
(which is kind of true). "What was it, a
love letter?" I add.

"No, Tom, it wasn't. I've missed out on something.
Come on, we better go," she tells me.

"**M**ake the most of me being NICE,"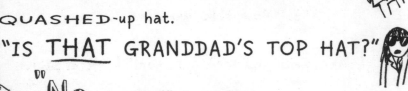
Delia tells me, before she <u>SPOTS</u> the

SQUASHED-up hat.

"IS <u>THAT</u> GRANDDAD'S TOP HAT?"

"**N**o ... YES!" I splutter.

"You're going to be in trouble now.

How did you do it, Tom?"

"I don't know — stuff just happens," I sigh.

Now Dad starts calling us from downstairs.

"HURRY UP, YOU TWO!"

"Come on, Tom, we'd better go. Tell them it was an

accident," Delia says to me.

"**B**UT IT **WAS** an ACCIDENT!" I say.

"I'm sure it's **NO big** deal that you squashed up

a PRECIOUS family heirloom..."

(Delia's enjoying this.)

"THERE you both are! We have to get Granddad to the wedding. We can't be LATE," Dad tells us.

"LOVE the suit, Tom! Very creative," Granddad tells me. "You look lovely too, Delia." Granddad smiles. "The ONLY thing that's missing is my LUCKY TOP HAT. Is it back from the cleaners?" Granddad asks us.

(I gulp...)

Gulp

"I think Tom might be able to help you with the hat." Delia gives me a shove forward.

"I'm sorry, Granddad, it was an accident," I say and bring out the hat.

Dad and Granddad have a LONG

S I L E N T

look at it...

Oh dear.

"How did that happen?" Dad asks.

"Delia sat on it!"

I say and she goes CRAZY.

TOM! Don't you dare!

"OK, it was me. I sat on it, but I'm really sorry,"
I tell them quickly.

"I can see why you were so worried, Tom,
but there was no need," Granddad says.
"All you had to do was ... THIS."
Granddad puts his hand inside the
hat and sort of BASHES it back out.

Like MAGIC it pops back
into shape.

Tah Dah!

"WOW! You mean I could have done that all this
time?" I ask.

"That's right, Tom! That's how we kept it in the family for all these years. Shall we go? I don't want to keep Mavis waiting. Another **FIFTY YEARS OF JOY AWAITS!**" Granddad LAUGHS.

Delia asks to take a few photos before we go, though surprisingly she doesn't smile very much.

"Everyone LOOK UP!" she tells us.

"And, Tom ... I can see what you're doing."

(Ha! Ha! Bunny ears.)

THE LEAFY GREEN OLD FOLKS' HOME

looks very fancy. Everywhere's been decorated with streamers and balloons for the wedding. **Teacup Tony and the Saucers** have set up their equipment ready to play. Uncle Kevin, Aunty Alice and the cousins are already here waiting for us.

"You're running late," Uncle Kevin says, tapping his watch.

"The 1970s suit you, Kevin," Dad tells him. The cousins look happy (not). They're not keen on their bow ties.

When the wedding starts, it's more **FUN** than I was expecting. We all have kazoos on our seats and we have to play "Here Comes the Bride" as Granny Mavis...

I'm here!

*R*ollerblades down the aisle at SPEED.

Mum whispers, "She chose the bat-winged dress especially to make an entrance."

"Impressive..." I agree.

(My granny's a legend – they both are.)

A lady called AGNES helps them renew their vows, and she compliments everyone on excellent kazoo playing.

Agnes has a large pineapple hat on her head, which is a bit distracting.

Granny and Granddad say their vows, then both read out poems. I find myself looking at Agnes's hat more than listening to what's going on.

I start blowing my kazoo at the wrong time until Mum nudges me.

BuZZZZ
BuZZZZ

Then everyone cheers and claps as The Fossils are married all over again.

It's doubly great that **DOGZOMBIES** are playing at the party as well. **AND** Granny said I could invite a few of my friends. (So I did.)

Norman has already arrived and made himself at home by the buffet.

AMY and **D**erek are there too.

"Excellent doodled suit, Tom," she tells me.

"Nice biscuits as well!"

Norman says with his mouth full.

"**Miss WAFER** offered to donate them after she spoke to Mum and Dad about my doodles," I explain happily. Although looking at **N**orman, I think he might have eaten half of them already.

"Hey, **N**orman, are you going to be OK to play the drums?" **D**erek wonders (because **N**orman and sugar don't mix).

"Sure, I'll be fine!" he tells us and then starts spinning around.

WEEEEEEEEE!

(Which is not good sign.)

And there's another problem looming...

Teacup Tony and the Saucers are due to start

playing and get the party started. BUT he's asleep.

ZZZZZZZZZZZZZZZ

"Tony's peaked already – he's gone

for a power nap, and the DJs not here

yet, either," says Dad, who looks a bit

concerned.

"Maybe **DOGZOMBIES** could play a few songs early?"

Mum suggests, looking at me.

"We'll do it!" I say. "We've still got the kazoos

– we can all join in."

"I'm ready NOW!"

Norman shouts, and runs over to the drum kit

(which is a worry).

CRASH

CRASH

WALLOP

(Uh-oh...)

BANG

BANG

BANG

Teacup
Tony and the
Saucers

"Sorry. I think I'm a bit HYPER.

I might go and drink some water,"

Norman tells us. (It's a good idea.)

"I can play the kazoo, again," AMY suggests.

"Thanks, AMY, but we really need a drummer.

We'll have to wait for Norman to calm down,"

Derek says.

"Come on, Tom – now's your chance. Can you play

something when your grandparents walk in?" Mum

asks me. "They'll be here soon." I can – but I need

to be quick as Uncle Kevin has overheard us, and

looks KEEN to join in. But as we're

discussing what to play...

Uh-oh...

Delia sits down at the drum kit.

"For goodness' sake, I'm SURROUNDED by

idiots," she says and only starts to play the

drums REALLY WELL!

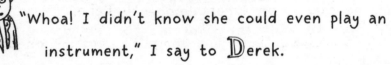
"Whoa! I didn't know she could even play an

instrument," I say to Derek.

"Me neither," he agrees.

"She's good," AMY adds.

Mum and Dad look surprised too.

"She kept that quiet," Mum says. "We're such a

musical family!"

"Like the Partridge Family." Dad LAUGHs.

THE FOSSILS make an entrance while Delia plays an **EXCELLENT** drumroll.

Then **D**erek and I start singing the Biscuit Song
with **AMY** on kazoo, and (I can't believe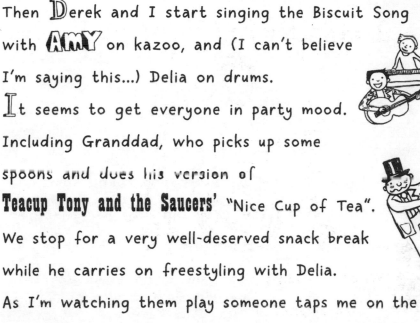
I'm saying this...) Delia on drums.

It seems to get everyone in party mood.

Including Granddad, who picks up some

spoons and does his version of

Teacup Tony and the Saucers' "Nice Cup of Tea".

We stop for a very well-deserved snack break

while he carries on freestyling with Delia.

As I'm watching them play someone taps me on the

shoulder.

 "Is that Delia on the drums?" a bloke asks.

"It is ... I had no idea she could play like

that," I tell him.

"I did - but I've not seen her play live before.

She's really good," he says. I look up and suddenly

realize WHO he is.

It's the bloke who came to see Delia!

"What are you doing at my grandparent's wedding?"
I wonder.

"I'm your DJ. I'd better set up."

"Aren't you in a band?" I ask.

"Yeah, that's right. We asked Delia to join, but
she never got back to us. I dropped round some
band photos and a letter. You did give her that
envelope, didn't you?" the bloke wants to know.

"Yes, I did..." I tell him. "Eventually,"
I add really quietly.

"I'll see if I can catch up with her later. Better get
the **1970s disco** going!" he tells me.

Looking at the cousins I can tell
they can't wait.

W e all have a really good time

SINGING,  DANCING

AND EATING.

I'm EXTRA pleased that everything's all sorted
with the **DOODLE WALL** now.

Mum's happy with her dress,
Granddad's top hat is all fine, and even Delia's
smiling (nearly) as it looks like she could be
joining her own band too.

I've never heard of most of the songs the DJ is
playing, but I think NOW might be a good time to
ask him for a VERY special request...

CONGRATULATIONS TO BOB AND MAVIS

"This song goes out to DELIA, as it's her favourite band EVER.
So here's a little bit of
ONE DIMENSION
just for her..."

Smiley face

(Well, I thought it was FUNNY...)

TOM!

A few weeks later...

I'm walking home from school with Derek and we're discussing IMPORTANT things – like why does Mrs Nap still insist on singing the register?

When we walk round the corner and see...

MY DOODLES on the
BISCUIT POSTER.

Which looks **SPECTACULAR!**

How to Make a Simple KAZOO

You will need:

2 x wooden lolly sticks OR

2 x craft wooden sticks

1 x THICK elastic band

2 x thin elastic bands

2 x small pieces of paper 5cm 5cm

Sticky tape - 2 x small pieces, looped over

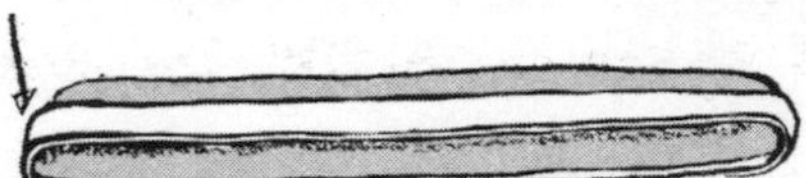

1) Take your wooden stick and stretch
the THICK elastic band over it.

2) Fold both pieces of paper in half  and then in half again and AGAIN and AGAIN.

Your two bits of paper should look like this.

3) Put your sticky tape loops on each bit of paper and stick them on your stick, one on TOP of the elastic band

under

and the other UNDER the elastic band.

4) Pop the other stick on TOP of the paper, then wrap the thin elastic bands around each end nice and tightly.

Make sure there's a bit of space to BLOW through.

AND IT'S READY!

RASP!

MY sad face, happy face DOODLE 😊

MAKE YOUR OWN CONGRATULATIONS CARD!

Trace or copy this design and fill in the spaces
with your own message.

GUESS WHO?

I went to a REAL BISCUIT factory and it <u>WAS</u> SPECTACULAR, even though I had to wear this. So now you know where ideas come from.

Liz  is the author-illustrator of several picture books. Tom Gates is the first series of books she has written and illustrated for older children. They have won several prestigious awards, including the Roald Dahl Funny Prize, the Waterstones Children's Book Prize, and the Blue Peter Book Award. The books have been translated into forty-five languages worldwide.

Visit her at www.LizPichon.com

Coming soon
to a foot near you!

A **BRAND** new story that features
FANTASTIC footwear
with **GADGETS**.

FEARLESS,
funny characters –
Ruby and Bear Foot.

A **FURIOUS** baddie
who'll stop at **NOTHING**
to get her hideous hands
and horrible feet into
the **ULTIMATE**
AWARD-WINNING shoe.

Welcome to **SHOE TOWN** and...

Published in the UK by Scholastic Children's Books, 2020
Euston House, 24 Eversholt Street, London, NW1 1DB, UK
A division of Scholastic Limited.

London – New York – Toronto – Sydney – Auckland
Mexico City – New Delhi – Hong Kong

SCHOLASTIC and associated logos are trademarks and/or
registered trademarks of Scholastic Inc.

First published in hardback by Scholastic Ltd, 2019

Text and illustrations © Liz Pichon Ltd, 2019

The right of Liz Pichon to be identified as the author and illustrator of this work
has been asserted by her under the Copyright, Designs and Patents Act 1988.

ISBN 978 1407 18673 3

A CIP catalogue record for this book is available from the British Library.

Printed by CPI Group (UK) Ltd, Croydon, CR0 4YY
Papers used by Scholastic Children's Books are made
from wood grown in sustainable forests.

1 3 5 7 9 10 8 6 4 2

This is a work of fiction. Names, characters, places, incidents
and dialogues are products of the author's imagination or are used
fictitiously. Any resemblance to actual people, living or dead,
events or locales is entirely coincidental.

www.scholastic.co.uk